I0710078
THE LAST PIECE
LAST
PIECE
DONALD F. AVERILL

INK START MEDIA
265 Eastchester Dr Ste 133 #102
High Point NC 27262

THE LAST PIECE

DONALD F. AVERILL

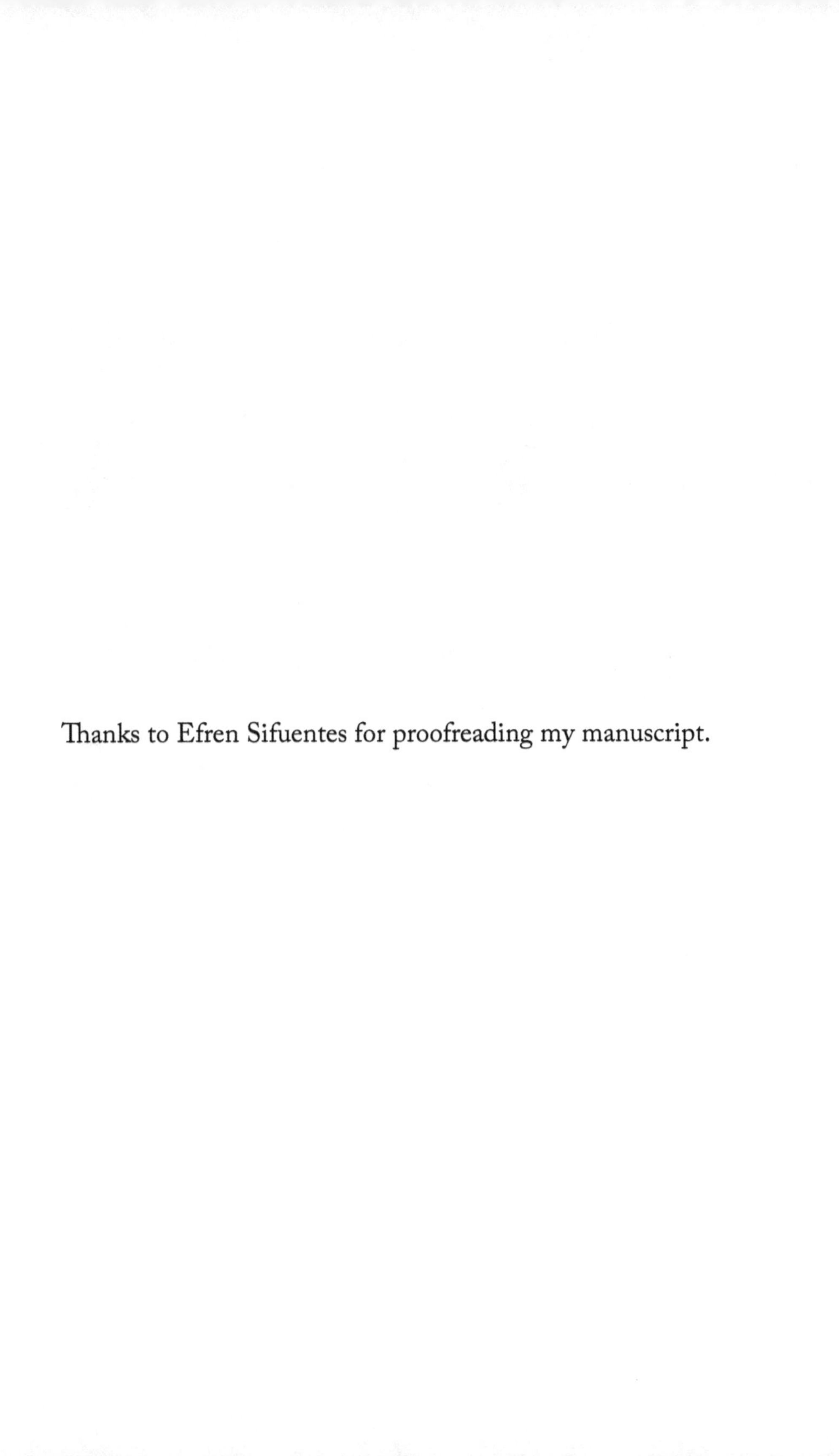

Thanks to Efren Sifuentes for proofreading my manuscript.

CHAPTER 1

It was an early afternoon in the second week of September, a chilly Friday but not unusual for the 6,131 foot elevation of Summit's Way, Colorado. I was grocery shopping at the nearest low-cost supermarket, only six minutes from home. I hadn't seen any acquaintances in the store for the entire half hour I pushed that detestable cart up and down aisle after aisle. One of the wheels caused that cussed grocery truck to drift to the right as I sought the items on my list. Two hands pushing was the only solution to the straying shopping wagon. I was glad the wheels didn't squeak, that would have been the last straw. I spent several minutes touring the passageways looking for my husband's requested item, canned tuna for his lunchtime sandwiches. I finally asked one of the stock workers for directions.

The young man didn't bother to look up and said, "The far end of aisle K, on the right by the pillar." Then he briefly glanced at me and resumed slicing open several cardboard cartons with a box knife. I think he was still in high school, working at a temporary job, not interested in climbing the ladder for permanent employment.

"Thank you." I turned my cart around and retraced my steps. I was already in aisle K. I had passed by the stacked cans, certainly not at the height I would have easily noticed.

What I needed, wouldn't you know, was on the lowest shelf, a few inches off the floor. So, I had to get on my hands and knees to retrieve four cans of hopefully, low mercury, low salt, packed in water tuna fish. As I held onto the cart and struggled to my feet, I glanced down the aisle to see if anyone had noticed my posterior jutting into the air. Kneeling was not a problem but getting back up was a bit of a chore.

The thought of signing up for a class in water aerobics briefly flitted through my mind. I was going to force myself to eat smaller portions and cut out desserts—completely. Frank might join me and lose some weight too. A change in diet might help him improve his golf game. That was going to be my strategy, something we could do together; that is lose weight, not play golf. Golf is not at all interesting to me. Chasing a ball around is not my idea of fun, that's for a dog.

I exited the checkout line with three reusable bags full of packaged foods after swiping my new Visa credit card through the handy little unit that displayed my total of $83.17. The sacker loaded the bags into the wounded cart and I was on my way out the door. The wind had picked up since I arrived at the store and dark clouds approached. My car was located about thirty yards from the entrance, adjacent to a cart return site. Hoping I could get the groceries in the car and my Chevy back on the street heading home before the rain arrived were the only things I had planned for the next five minutes.

My shopping bags contained no fragile items so I hurriedly tossed them on the floor behind my seat. I slammed the back door, opened the driver's door and climbed into the car just as a drop of rain struck my forehead. With the seatbelt latched, I started the engine and shifted into reverse with my foot on the brakes. I'm glad I looked at the back view on the screen because a bright red vehicle was in my way and honking. What was their problem? A firetruck blocked my way but why was the driver honking at me? A few raindrops struck the windshield so I set my wipers on slow and took another look at the vehicle behind me.

The driver was getting out. I expected to see a large man in uniform, but it was a woman, about my size in a house dress. I twisted in my seat, put my window down and stuck my head out to see if I could recognize her. I was shocked, it was one of my bridge buddies, Dorothy Higgins. What was she doing driving one of those small firetrucks? I thought those vehicles were for the big honchos that ran the show at fires or pushed pencils back at the station.

"Hi Marilee!" She shouted.

"Hi Dotty! What are you doing driving a firetruck?"

"Oh! That's not a firetruck, that's our new car. Dale repossessed it and we bought it from the bank. Let me park. I have something to tell you. Don't go anywhere, just a sec."

I watched Dotty scramble into her tank and park the beast four cars to my left. She exited the suburban holding a grocery bag over her head and came running to the passenger side of my car. I pressed the unlock button, she slid into the passenger seat and pulled the door shut.

"Whew! The rain is getting heavier. I had my hair done yesterday and wanted to stay home today, but Dale wanted me to pick up a few things. There's a four day weekend coming up. The weathergirl on channel six said it was going to rain for the next couple of days. Oh, well, I'm glad I saw you. I was going to call when I got home."

Dotty took some deep breaths. I waited a couple of seconds and asked, "So what have you got to tell me?"

"You aren't going to believe this. Evelyn and Raymond Meyers are getting a divorce."

"What? I talked with Evie a couple of days ago and she didn't say anything about troubles with Ray. Something drastic must have happened all of a sudden. Did you talk with her?"

"No, Sheri told me."

"How did Sheri find out?"

"Mrs. Toliver said she heard them arguing."

"I don't know anyone by that name. Who is Mrs. Toliver?"

"That's Evelyn's elderly neighbor across the street."

"So, this is all hearsay. Let's not spread this around until we talk to Evie. You know how gossip can be damaging to everyone involved. I'll call Evie when I get home. If I find out anything, I'll text you or send an email. Okay?"

"Yes. I'll be expecting a message from you." Dotty gave me that look, *'I'll kill you if you don't tell me what's going on with Eve and Ray.'* She moved to open the door saying, "I've got to get in the store and pick up a few items. I'm making cookies and muffins today. I'm nearly out of flour and vanilla." She popped the door and stepped out into the rain, holding a grocery bag over her recent hairdo. Before she got the door closed, I said, "I'll get you the scuttlebutt later."

I watched her rush into the store as she tried to protect her hair from the rain. I set the wipers on a higher speed, checked for traffic behind me and backed out. The rain was coming down heavily and there was a loud clap of thunder which sounded close. I ducked my head and then laughed at my futile reaction.

About six or seven minutes later, I was in the garage unloading. When I opened the door to the mudroom, Blemish, my cat, and Fred, our Yorkie, greeted me. My husband, Frank, and I visited the local animal shelter about a year ago and came home with a cat and dog. Fred kept his name but the kitten hadn't been named. She was all white except for a dime sized black patch on her right ear, therefore Frank and I called her Blemish. Not a very flattering moniker, but appropriate.

The pets knew from past experience that I was coming home with groceries and they would be given a treat. They weren't wrong. Blemish was on top of the clothes washer and Fred was at my feet unconsciously trying to trip me. I nudged the little guy with my right foot, "Back, buddy, I don't want to step on you."

As soon as I got the bags on the counter, I gave Fred a treat. He scampered away to his bed to hide his prize in his blanket for later munchies. Blemish rubbed against my ankles and gave a little meow. Fortunately, each pet disliked the other's treats. I prepared Blemish's dinner before I got busy with Frank's and mine. Fred always ate after the rest of the family finished their meal and dessert.

When Frank got home from the office, he announced, "I'll be in there in a minute. I want to hear all about your day." Frank was in charge of Summit Way's main post office in Jefferson County, Colorado. I knew his routine when coming home Friday night. He would go into the bedroom, take off his shirt and tie and put on his bedroom slippers. I heard the rumble of the closet door sliding open and pictured him donning his worn out bathrobe. I'm planning to get him a new robe for his retirement, a little over a year away. I wanted to get him a new one now, but he made me promise not to replace that revered item for another year. I'm not sure why he made me give my word but I decided not to harp on it. I'm not the nagging type, but sometimes . . . I can reach the end of my rope.

Frank came into the kitchen carrying Fred but the little guy wanted down, so Frank changed one type of cuddling for another, he put his arms around my waist and nuzzled my neck as I was trying to get some eggs from the refrigerator. I turned into him, gave him a peck on the cheek and said, "Evelyn and Raymond are getting a divorce."

"What! That can't be right. Where did you hear that? I saw Ray at the bank on Tuesday and he didn't mention anything like that to me. He would have said something."

"I saw Dotty at the market. She told me. I told Dotty I would check on it with Eve tonight after dinner. I have to call her about something else anyway."

"So, Dotty got it directly from Eve?"

"No, Mrs. Toliver told a guy named Stanley. Stan told Sheri. Sheri told Dotty."

"Jeez Marilee, that sounds like one of those kid's games where something is said secretly to one kid and repeated umpteen times to others and the last kid in line says something completely different from the original. I think you're right; you should talk to Eve yourself." He pulled out a dining room chair and asked, "Are we out of beer?"

"Nope, we're going on a diet."

"Not again! Was that a suggestion from Dorothy? Has she got Dale trying to slim down? He could stand to lose a few pounds, like twenty or thirty."

"No, it wasn't Dotty. It was my own idea after I got your tuna off the bottom shelf at the Red and White Market. I felt like a hippo when I got on my hands and knees."

"Come on, Mar. You aren't fat. But I guess I could lose a few. Might help with my golf swing."

"That's what I thought. We can do it together ... lose a few pounds."

"I'm changing the subject. What have you planned for dinner?"

"Tuna casserole and a green salad with thousand Island dressing—low calorie."

"And dessert?"

"I haven't thought that far ahead. We still have some ice cream but no chocolate sauce."

"You're going to force me to have a bedtime snack . . . half a peanut butter sandwich." Frank grinned.

"Well, all right but no jam."

We didn't eat until 6:30 and it was uneventful. We talked about our day and after dessert, Frank put the dishes in the machine while I called Evelyn. The bridge club member's numbers were saved in my phone so I speed-dialed Evie.

She answered after the first ring. "*Hi Marilee, what's going on?*"

"That was quick! You must have been holding your phone. Were you about to call someone?"

"No, I just wanted to recharge the battery and I picked up the phone to plug it in to the charger."

I chuckled, "I have two questions for you. Number one is about next week's club meeting. It is supposed to be at your house. Do you still want to host it?"

"Yes, I do. Why are you wondering?"

"Well, I heard you and Ray are getting a divorce. You might not want us girls around during the turmoil."

Eve started laughing, *"Where did you hear such craziness? Ray and I aren't having any problems."*

"Dotty said Sheri told her that Mrs. Toliver heard you guys raising your voices about getting a divorce. You were having a big argument."

"Mrs. Toliver? Oh my gosh. She needs hearing aids. The only thing I can remember saying regarding a divorce was about my cousin's daughter. Erin is suing Doug for a divorce. They've been separated for six months and he's not paying child support for their two kids. I'll bet Mrs. Toliver heard me yelling at Ray when he was down in the basement. He was cutting some plywood with his jigsaw and I had to shout at him. I suppose I should have waited until he finished making all that racket. He's making some Christmas lawn decorations from plywood."

"That's good to hear. Frank and I couldn't imagine you and Ray were having trouble, so I had to call and get the facts."

"Well, tomorrow's Saturday, so I'll visit with Rose and set her straight. She's a dear old soul and does gardening on Saturday. Almost all of her close neighbors drop by to say hello to see how she's doing. She's in her nineties."

"Was she ever married?"

"Sure, three times. She divorced or outlived them all. Mrs. Toliver was a librarian for more than fifty years. She helped many interesting people. That's where she met her husbands, they visited the library."

CHAPTER 2

I got off the phone with Evelyn after promising to call Sheri to clue her in about the divorce rumors concerning the Meyers. It was ten to eight when I dialed Sheri. Her husband, Tom, answered. He has a deep baritone voice. You would think he was an enormous man, but he's a skinny five-foot-seven nerd, wears glasses, and is slightly balding. Frank always jokes that God played a trick on Tom.

"Hello. If you're wanting me to answer a bunch of political crap, forget it."

"Hi Tom. This is Marilee, no politics tonight. Can I talk to Sheri?"

"Sure. She's fighting with the clothes washer. Just a sec, I'll get her for you."

I waited for about a minute—an exceptionally long second— before Sheri picked up the phone and answered. *"Hi Marilee. Did you find out anything about Eve and Ray?"*

"Yes. I just got off the phone with her. The divorce is a bunch of nonsense. Mrs. Toliver misinterpreted what she heard. Eve's cousin's daughter is getting a divorce. Her husband is a scumbag that is delinquent on his child support payments."

"That's good to know . . . I mean Eve's not getting a divorce. So, we're still having our get together on Tuesday?"

"Yes. We'll get caught up on every bit of news then."

"Okay, see you on Tuesday at one o'clock. Bye."

I punched the OFF button and leaned back in the sofa thinking of Tom's reaction when I called. He must have recently gotten off the phone with one of those political survey questionnaires, obviously not his cup of tea.

Frank was updating his stamp collection with new issues while I was on the phone. He was the only husband of the bridge club members that was a collector. Not one of the other men, or their wives had been blessed with the collector's gene. When I got off the phone, he joined me from his stamp room, previously our daughter's nursery.

He was smiling, "Are we going to have some dessert or am I going to have to suffer new diet pains?"

I stood between him and the refrigerator. I anticipated what he was going to ask. I was ready. "We've got ice cream or apple pie. There's not much pie, we're down to the last wedge. I had a sliver of it at noon."

We stood there looking at each other. I waited for a suggestion, but for only a few seconds.

He pulled out one of the dining table chairs. "Okay. Let's have the pie with ice cream on top. Put it on a large plate and we'll split it. Grab two forks."

"That's a great idea! That will be the first dessert of our new diet project."

"Any coffee left?"

"Sure, I'll heat it up."

I turned on the coffee maker and stuck the pie in the microwave for thirty seconds to warm it up.

Frank scooted back the chair and was resting his elbows on the dining room table when he suddenly asked, "How did Donny's operation go? Did Linette update you about our grandson?"

"Uh-huh. I got a text from her before I went to the store. She said the operation went perfectly . . . according to the doctor. He will have to wear a bandage for about a month, but his ears won't stick out from his head like they used to."

"That's good. He's gone through a lot of teasing and bullying over the last three years. He told me it was mostly older boys. His classmates never call him Dumbo, elephant ears, or ask him when he is going to fly. I know what teasing is like. When I was his age, maybe a few years younger, I was a little chubby and a few kids called me fatty, chubs or piggy. When they chose members of teams at recess, I was nearly always one of the last picks."

"Linette told me about him being teased. He didn't cry, but when he told her about it, she could see the tears. Older boys can be very mean. It's not the smart kids that give him trouble, it's the stupid ones. But since he will be in the same building as the older boys, Linette wanted to have his ears pulled back before he goes to junior high in the high school building."

I mused, "There seems to be quite a few older lamebrains. Too bad they don't have smarter parents. It's no wonder sensitive kids commit suicide."

The skinny piece of pie didn't last long, only a few bits of crust remained. Frank wet his right index finger and poked at the tiny remaining morsels and licked off his finger, something his father used to do. I think that was a leftover from the depression years. His family didn't have much, but his father made sure his children were properly fed and nothing went to waste. Our warmed over coffee lasted longer than the pie. I had squirted a blob of whipped cream on the reheated liquid, just to surprise Frank. He purposely tipped his mug up to form a white mustache on his upper lip. We enjoyed a good laugh before exhausting tidbits of conversation and readying for bed. We didn't bother with the small number of dishes.

Frank was already in bed when I finished some touch-up work on my face in the bathroom. I saw his can of shaving cream and thought one of these days I would use it instead of whipped cream on his dessert. I'll wait until I'm sure he's in a good mood. If we stick to a diet plan, it might be awhile before I buy another pie. A homemade pie might be better, I could lessen the caloric content. I'll find a recipe and make some changes, use some artificial sweetener instead of sugar. The bridge club will be my guinea pigs before I subject Frank to a low-cal pie. But I can't remember him ever complain about my cooking.

Saturday was a sleep-in morning. It was around nine o'clock when I heard the neighbor's lawn mower interrupt my dream. I was back in high school in chemistry class and couldn't understand anything the teacher was saying as he directed our attention to the periodic table with his laser pointer. I opened my eyes and saw Frank, still sleeping. I sat up and rubbed my eyelids, suddenly back to reality. I put on my slippers and made a quick trip to the porcelain palace, Frank's designation for the bathroom.

As I went to the kitchen to get breakfast started, I heard Frank ask from the bedroom, "Do you know who lives at 703 Summit Street?"

I guess he was up and getting dressed. He must have heard me moving around. I answered, "That's that small blue house with white trim, isn't it?"

"I don't know what color it is. I don't recall that address. They're having a garage sale today. I saw a pink sign as I was driving home from work. I'm gonna check it out—see if they have anything worthwhile."

Frank came into the kitchen blinking his eyes and stretching his arms. He was dressed in a tee shirt and jeans, very unprofessional for a postal employee that wears a suit every day of the work week. He looked relaxed. He came over to me and circled me with his arms.

"Whatcha got cookin'?"

"Your favorite, blueberry pancakes and bacon. Get your hairy arms off me and set the table, please. There's OJ in the fridge."

He released me but kissed the back of my neck. I attempted to swat him with my spatula but he moved quickly beyond my reach.

"You'd better be careful; I'll report domestic abuse and you'll be kept from your bridge game on Tuesday." He laughed and then said, "What are your plans while I'm looking for some cheap stuff at that garage sale?"

"I think I'll go over to Evie's and accompany her to talk with her elderly neighbor, Mrs. Toliver. Kind of investigate what it's going to be like when I'm in my nineties." I stacked three pancakes on a plate and handed it to Frank.

"Thank you. Boy those look good! Are you having some, too?"

"Nope. Toast and grapefruit for me. Starting today I'm cutting down on butter and syrup."

Frank raised his right eyebrow, took a bite of pancakes, swallowed, and responded. "You're really serious about this diet thing, aren't you?"

"I am serious. I noticed Dorothy's flat stomach today and figured I'd better get busy on some personal improvements. I was hoping you would join me to improve your physical fitness. Don't you think better health would help improve your golf game?"

He gave me a serious look, speared the last bite of pancake and washed it down with a swig of coffee. "You're right, Marilee. No more pancakes on Saturdays but I'm not a fan of grapefruit."

"I'll get you a box of raisin bran. How about that?"

"Better not. Raisins give me nasty gas. Better make it Rice Chex or Rice Crispies—I'll top them off with sliced bananas. Oh, better get some 2% or non-fat milk."

"All right. It sounds like you're going to join me in this crusade."

"Yep! Circle the wagons. We'll take on the excess sugar and fat. Let's get another more accurate scale for the bathroom. Maybe a digital one. See if you can find one that has memory and printout capabilities."

I began to feel that Frank was trying to make this an expensive undertaking and hoping I would back off because of the exorbitant cost. I was going to fool him and follow just what he recommended. I doubted that I could find what he suggested, so as I was getting into his car, I decided to try something else. I was taking his car and he was taking mine, the SUV, in case he had to haul something large from the garage sale.

Frank stayed behind to check on the animals before leaving for the sale. I drove directly to the only antique store in town. If I could find what I wanted, I was positive it would fit in the backseat of the car. My only concern was the item might be expensive since it was an antique. When I entered the store the door triggered a bell. I felt like I was visiting a shop from a century earlier. There was little organization but lots of little signs to aid in searches. I noticed two men were present, one seemed to be the proprietor next to an old fashioned cash register and the other a customer looking at some tools.

I doubted if there was anything digital in the store unless the owner used a calculator for totaling sales plus tax. If I couldn't find what I wanted, I'd visit a department store and hit the bedroom/bathroom sections. I might get lucky and find a scale like the one Frank suggested. If it is too expensive, I can always return it after Frank objects to the cost.

I ambled over to the counter and asked, "Do you have one of those old fashioned business scales that people could weigh themselves for a penny or a nickel?"

The clerk smiled, showing a mouth of crooked teeth. He wiped his hands on a wadded blue and white plaid handkerchief, stuffed it back in his back right pants' pocket, and answered, "I do have one of those. As soon as I help this gentleman, I'll show it to you. It's in my back storage room."

While I waited, I watched the counterman. He was a bit taller than my Frank, probably six-one or so, wore a bright yellow shirt and tan pants. He came from behind the counter and led his customer to the back corner of the establishment. He looked comfortable wearing white sneakers. I couldn't help but glance around the room to see if there was anything small I could pilfer, if it was something I really needed. My mind was wandering, it was only a brief thought; I wouldn't stoop so low. I have never shoplifted. I imagined the headlines: "Wife of postmaster caught taking candy from local store. Postmaster resigns in disgrace."

The customer paid for his items and left the building. Mr. Tan pants motioned for me to follow him. The far back, poorly lighted region of the building was a storage area for various items, some of which I couldn't identify. The strange items were on a large table in front of several larger pieces, three or four picture frames that looked older than dirt, and just what I was seeking, a weighing machine. I could see it used pennies; ideal for Frank and me. I could get several rolls from the bank. They would be constantly recycled.

Todd, I noticed his name was displayed on his shirt pocket, saw that I recognized the machine and asked, "Is that what you are looking for?"

"Yes, but I can't pay that much for it." I saw the tag with $600 written on it.

CHAPTER 3

"Oh! That tag doesn't mean anything. That's the price the previous owner listed for the item at auction. I can let it go for $250, including tax."

"Does it work, or is it just for decorative purposes?"

"It works but it's out of fortunes. They were specially printed on little paper cards, like business cards. A person's weight is displayed in pounds on the dial and the tick marks indicate ounces. Let me pull it out and show you." He smiled at me and said, "I've got a few pennies. I'll have to move the table first. The scale is quite heavy; I'll get a hand truck and if you want the scale, I'll load it for you."

I watched Todd move the table by rotating it so he could access the object with his hand truck. I felt like he was making a lot of extra effort to show me how it functioned. I had already decided to buy it. Frank would have to suffer the consequences and pay the credit card amount. With the scale off the hand truck so it was level, Todd stepped on the weighing platform, extracted a penny from his pocket and weighed himself. I was happy he didn't ask me to step on the scale.

"One eighty-five. That's probably right on. This morning, I weighed myself on my bathroom scale and it was 183 but that was without shoes, just slippers."

"Okay, I'll take it. Will you take a VISA card?"

"Not a problem. I take all cards, cash or checks."

As I paid for the scale, I imagined what Frank was going to say when he saw how much it cost, probably ten times the amount he would expect for a standard bathroom scale. But it would be a good talking point for visitors. I would leave some pennies on the top of the toilet for anyone to use. I expect we will be having an argument when he comes home. I'll have to have some help getting the damned thing out of the car.

"Are you driving a pickup or an SUV?"

"I have my husband's sedan. Can you put it in the back seat or the trunk?"

"It has to remain vertical or the weights will be jumbled; the whole thing would have to be taken apart and fixed. It can't be laid down. Let's measure the roof height behind the front seats, it might fit if the front seat is moved forward. If not, maybe you can come by tomorrow with a bigger vehicle."

Todd grabbed a tape measure and checked the height of the scale and then we went to the car to measure the distance from the floor to the ceiling. It would fit with an inch to spare. I watched him open the passenger side front door and slide the seat all the way forward. We went back in the store and wheeled the scale to the car. I couldn't do much but watch as Todd wrestled the heavy white machine inside the car.

"What do you think it weighs?"

Todd sighed and said, "About a hundred pounds; it's made of cast iron. Modern replicas are made from polymers and aluminum. They're much lighter."

Frank is a bigger man than Todd, so he probably won't have much trouble getting the scale out of his car. "Well, thanks for loading it. I'll be back for other things now that I've seen your whole store. I'll tell my friends what you have."

"Thank you Mrs. Neally. Enjoy the scale. Thanks for the business."

I climbed in the car, waved to Todd, looked at my purchase and smiled as I pulled away from the curb. I can hardly wait to see Frank's reaction. But first, I have to see what Evelyn is up to. She is going to have a talk with ancient Mrs. Toliver and I want to join them. I hope I'm not too late. I spent too much time at the antique store, but it was fun.

I was only a few minutes away from Evie's home, not far from the golf course. Ray would probably be home since the bank was closed on the weekend. I wouldn't be surprised if he was out in the backyard practicing with his putter. Frank said Ray had a green installed so he could improve his light strokes. We don't have the room or the funds to do that in our backyard. I wouldn't let Frank do it anyway. I can't think of a bigger waste of money. He can practice at the golf course or wait for an invitation from Ray. Besides, we would, without doubt, have to buy a new mower to cut the grass really short and a special tool to install the hole in the green. Ray probably has everything to take care of his backyard putting surface, including a flag. Fortunately, Frank has his stamp collection and playing golf does not top his list of pastimes.

I pulled in beside Ray's black BMW in the Meyers' driveway and beeped my horn . . . only once so not to alarm Evie or Ray. Evie came out the front door smiling and waving. She had on a pair of gray pants and a large, long-sleeve shirt, undoubtedly one of Ray's.

She greeted me as I got out of the car, "Hi Marilee. Who is the little person in the back seat?" She turned her head as she crouched to see through the rear window. "Oh, that's not a person. What is that?"

I had to laugh. "It's a scale I picked up at the antique store. Frank and I are starting our new diet. We're going to lose some baggage we've been accumulating the last few years. I want to get a flat stomach again."

"And Frank is going along with this?"

"Yep." I nodded. "We think it will improve his golf game. What's Ray doing today?"

"He's puttering around with something out in back." She motioned with her right thumb.

"Don't you mean putting?"

"No," she smiled, "he's doing something with the lawn mower . . . he thinks it has a clogged filter. It won't start."

I had to ask about Mrs. Toliver. I wondered if Evie had gone to see her today. "Have you talked with your elderly neighbor this morning?"

"Not yet. Come with me and I'll introduce you."

"Am I interrupting something? Were you going to do some gardening?"

She glanced down at her attire and commented, "This is my usual garb for doing housework. I was going to clean the drapes and vacuum under beds today but I can do that later. Let's see if we can find Mrs. Toliver."

Evie started walking toward the street motioning me to join her. I quickened my stride and caught up halfway across the asphalt. There was no indication of yesterday's downpour, the road was as dry as a new sack of flour. We walked across the grass to the front door and Evie knocked almost violently. I assumed Evie's attack was due to Mrs. Toliver's hearing difficulty. She would surely react to her door and walls vibrating.

We waited, exchanging smiles, shrugs and uneasiness expressed in facial contortions for what seemed five minutes but was actually about a minute before the door opened. Mrs. Toliver appeared wearing a questioning look. "May I help you young ladies?" There was a moment of silence and then she said, "Oh, you are Evelyn from across the street."

I was mentally jolted by her greeting. Evie and I are both over sixty. Young ladies was certainly not an accurate description of us.

Evelin spoke with her volume turned up, "Mrs. Toliver, I would like you to meet a friend of mine, Marilee Neally. Her husband runs the post office."

The old woman and I exchanged niceties and she commented, "Rufus, my second husband, was a stamp collector but he only collected the stamps of Great Britain. He loved studying watermarks and plate numbers. He bought lots of stamps at foreign auctions, mostly from Canada and England."

I didn't know anything about collecting stamps; that was Frank's hobby and I never showed much interest in it. I think that was a mistake. I asked, "Did you collect, too?"

"Oh, as a kid, but he used to explain everything to me. I read through one of the catalogs at the library. There are many ways to collect stamps. I kept some of his things: tongs, perforation gauges and a nice watermark detector."

All I could do was grin and nod. What she said seemed correct. I didn't understand half of her comments. I'll have to ask Frank about his collection. I felt a bit embarrassed, not knowing but a slight amount about stamp collecting. Then Evie suggested, "Can we go somewhere to sit and talk, Mrs. Toliver?"

"Why sure, I would like that. I've got a nice place out back. I think you'll like my roses."

Evie and I followed Mrs. Toliver through the house into the backyard. There was a large awning extending over her back porch, where a rectangular glass top table and four chairs rested. She stood at the slider and asked, "Would you like a spot of tea?"

I glanced at Evie and she replied, "Yes, that would be nice."

Mrs. Toliver disappeared for a couple of minutes. As we waited for her return, Evie said, "I think she must have spent some time in England."

That was my thought exactly after hearing *a spot of tea* emitted from Mrs. Toliver.

Our conversation was interrupted by a man's voice. "Why are you ladies almost yelling at Mrs. Toliver?"

It was a next door neighbor holding a rake. He stood on the other side of a hurricane fence. Evie replied in a normal voice, "Mrs. Toliver is hard of hearing. We want her to understand what we are saying. Who are you, anyway?"

"I'm Stan Gaddins. I've lived here next to Rose Toliver for the last twelve years. I've talked with her innumerable times and never known her to be hard of hearing. I talked with Rose yesterday and she didn't have any trouble hearing my every word."

Evie and I looked at each other a little dismayed. I wondered if Mrs. Toliver was playing a prank. I was sure Evie had the same idea.

Evie said, "I think we've been hoodwinked, Marilee."

I began to laugh and Evie joined in.

"Did I miss out on a joke?" Mrs. Toliver interrupted our giggling as she exited her kitchen through the slider carrying a tray with cups, a pitcher, a saucer of sugar cubes and a small container of cream.

Evie smiled, "No, we just realized you have been putting us on about your hearing. We've been talking to your neighbor. He clued us in about your prank."

"I hope I haven't made enemies of you. I like to jest with people. It's something I picked up from living in England. I guess it isn't always appreciated. Do you mind my little sport?"

I replied after glancing at Evie. She gave a slight shrug and grinned. "We don't mind but we want to ask you about something."

Rose was pouring tea and listening closely. "What would you ladies like to know?"

Evie took the reins, "You have been telling people that my husband and I are getting a divorce. Why would you do that? Is that another of your jokes?" Evie sounded somewhat irritated. I wondered how Mrs. Toliver was going to react.

"You're not divorcing? That's not what I heard. I remember you yelling at your husband that you wanted a divorce. I heard you clear across the street."

Evie smiled, knowing exactly what Rose had overheard. "I was telling my husband that my cousin's daughter was getting a divorce. Ray was in the basement working with his jigsaw and I yelled at him so he could hear me. You didn't hear all that was said."

Rose asked, "Two lumps or just one?" glancing at both of us. I replied with none and Evie wanted two. My new diet had me cutting out extra sources of sugar.

"I'm sorry for misunderstanding, but as a result I got some visitors, didn't I?" she smiled. "I only told one person what I thought I heard, so don't be worried about rumors being spread around town. The grapevine isn't very fertile here."

I asked, "Who did you tell, Rose?" Evie and I both knew rumors could initiate with one person spreading the word.

She thought for a moment and quickly said, "Stanley. He's my neighbor. He knows Ray at the bank."

Evie looked at me and said, "Stan must know Sheri," and grinned. We had discovered the rumor's source.

Rose frowned and asked, "Who is Sheri?"

Realizing Mrs. Toliver didn't know our friends, I filled her in. I had to mention our bridge club when telling her about Dorothy Higgins and Sheri Sandborne and of course my cat, Blemish, and my little Yorkie, Fred.

Rose's excitement had taken over her entire being, her posture straightened, her checks flushed, and I noticed a new sparkle in her eyes. She was obviously interested in playing bridge. What was I going to do, tell her that we already had a foursome?

CHAPTER 4

I decided to ask her if she would like to come to our next bridge club meeting. I guess I should have consulted with Evie, Dotty, and Sheri first, but the idea just came to mind.

"Would you like to join our little group at our next get together?"

I glanced at Evie. She grinned and nodded. Her support lessened my anxiety.

"Oh, I would like that very much. Where and when?"

Evie joined in, "Tuesday, at my house, across the street, two o'clock. Don't bring anything. You can sit in as a partner for each one of us. That will allow you four hands. How does that sound?"

"That sounds wonderful. It's been a few years since I played, but I used to be rather good. My second husband and I won some tournaments when we lived in Philadelphia." She looked at her hands and thought for a moment. "My gosh, that was more than thirty years ago. I used to read the newspaper entertainment section for the bridge hands explanation and do the crossword puzzles. Those were great time passing activities when I was sitting at the library book checkout desk." Her eyes twinkled, "Lots of time to kill back then."

Chit-chat continued for a half hour. Then we heard a loud motor noise and Evie remarked, "I believe that's Ray's lawn mower. He must have discovered why the engine wouldn't start. I'll tell you something, when we were married, he was a total klutz—but over the years he has fixed all kinds of mechanical problems. He even repaired our dishwasher once. That saved us quite a bundle."

Rose glanced at me and inquired, "Is your husband handy with tools?"

I chuckled, "Kind of. He finds things at garage sales that are easily fixed. I can't remember when we bought our last new appliance. He's at a garage sale this morning. He'll bring something home he finds for a bargain price. It's surprising how many people get rid of things that still have plenty of life left in them. Some items just need a little doctoring."

I checked my watch and decided it was time to say goodbye to Rose and Evie. Evie stood with me and we thanked Rose for the tea and conversation. She followed us to the curb and as we walked back across the street, Rose yelled, "See you on Tuesday!"

Evie shouted as loudly as she could, "We'll see you on Tuesday!" We all were laughing as I got into my car. Evie waved to me as she started into the backyard to check on her husband; we could no longer hear the mower engine, maybe it ran out of gas.

As I backed out of the driveway, a glance at the dash clock indicated it was ten after eleven. Since I had to pass by Summit Street on the way home, I thought I'd pass by 703 and see if Frank was still there. But as I got closer to the sale location, I decided to pass by and not bother to look, too much time had lapsed since Frank left home. When I arrived at our drive, the SUV was parked at the curb. That hinted Frank didn't buy much or only a couple of small items, surely nothing big and heavy like the scale I purchased.

I drove up next to the kitchen entrance, shut off the engine and went inside. Frank would have to carry the scale into the house. I continued to wonder what his first impression would be.

"Frank?" I couldn't hear him but Fred came up to me and I bent over and scratched his scruff. "Where's your daddy?"

Little Fred cocked his head, looked at me and then turned and pranced over to the sliding patio door leading to the backyard. I followed him and sure enough, Frank was peering into a white metal tube mounted on a tripod.

"What *are* you doing?"

He chuckled, "I'm looking in our neighbors' windows."

"Really? Is that lawful? You bought a telescope?"

"Uh-huh. It's a good little scope for only twenty-five bucks. I'll have to buy some more eyepieces and filters though. It only has one eyepiece and it's not powerful enough for looking at planets, but it's good for peering in windows."

He stepped back, grinned and motioned for me to come closer. "Take a look."

I gradually lowered my eye to the eyepiece and saw something shiny but didn't know what it was. I knew it wasn't a neighbor's window. He was joking. I looked at Frank and he said, "Could you see it?"

I didn't know what 'it' was, so I asked, "What was I looking at?"

He smiled and said, "Look where the telescope is pointing. What do you see way off in the distance?"

I looked. "Those are trees!"

"Farther."

I shielded my eyes and squinted. I thought, what could that shiny thing be? I was stymied and glanced at Frank. I gave him a dumb look and he told me. "That's the top of the city water tower two miles away."

"Really?" I took another look. So that's what I was seeing so far away. Now I had the top of a water tower in my memory bank, something I had never seen before.

Frank started telling me about his purchase and afterwards, I told him about mine. "Come out to the car. The thing I bought is too heavy for me to carry in the house. I need your muscles." I chuckled and started around the house with Frank following a few paces behind. I used the remote entry button to unlock the back passenger door and swung the door open to expose the scale.

"What in the devil did you buy? This isn't what I wanted you to get. How much was it?"

"Two hundred and fifty dollars. It was a good deal. It works great but there aren't any fortunes."

Frank looked at it, gave me a scowling glance and said, "Okay, where do you want me to put it?"

I hadn't thought about a location, but it suddenly occurred to me, "In the hall alcove between the bedroom and the bathroom. We'll put a calendar on the wall and each morning after our bathroom visits we'll write down our weight. We have to be consistent or the weights won't mean anything. Do you think you can follow the routine?"

After a bit of grumbling in which I heard a "Yeah," he reached into the car, lifted the scale out and started toward the closest door, the entry to the kitchen. I rushed ahead and opened the door as wide as it would go. I didn't want him to bump the door jams and create dents in the woodwork. I watched him move through the kitchen and living room and into the hallway. His steps were getting shorter as he approached the bathroom. I think he was tiring of carrying the heavy object, but he made it to the alcove and set the scale down on the hallway rug. As soon as he stood up, I stepped past him and moved the little table from the recess to make room for my latest purchase.

Frank wrestled the scale into position and I stood there admiring the fixture. With his hands on his hips, he raised his eyebrows. It was obvious he was not pleased that I spent two hundred and fifty dollars on the piece. I knew he expected me to come home with a thirty dollar made in China object.

"I'll show you how it works. Do you have a penny?"

He laughed, "Sure," and reached into his right pants pocket and pulled out several coins. He held out his hand and I extracted a penny from about forty cents in coins in his palm. I stepped on the scale, inserted the penny into the slot and watched the indicator arm slowly climb past one hundred to one-forty. The indicator slowed to a crawl and came to rest on one hundred forty eight.

Frank whistled and I slugged his shoulder, not too hard.

I gave a little sneer, "Okay, you get on. I want to see if the scale goes far enough to register your weight."

He held out his hand to me to help me off the scale but I ignored the gesture. He stepped on the scale and said, "This baby will probably go to at least three hundred pounds. I'm not even close to that."

"If you don't have a penny, I'll get one from my purse."

"Don't bother, I've got another one but if we're going to do this every morning, you'll need to get some rolls of pennies from the bank."

"Why don't you get some at the post office? That will save me a trip downtown."

He shook his head, "I can't do that. Regulations won't allow us to use the post office as a personal bank."

I knew I had a several pennies in my change purse, so I said, "I've got a few pennies for Sunday and Monday morning weigh ins. I'll visit the bank Monday afternoon and get a couple of rolls. Todd told me he didn't have a money container key and didn't know how to get the coins from the machine. Maybe you can figure it out so we can recycle the pennies."

"Sounds like a plan. I'll check on the Internet and see if I can get some tidbits. Someone must know how to get the money out of the scale. The pennies aren't sealed in an impenetrable vault. I'll bet I can get it open with a screwdriver."

"Or you can call Ray, he fixed his lawnmower today."

"You were at the Meyers' today? I didn't think you were serious about seeing Eve. What were they up to?"

"Evie and I went across the street to talk with Mrs. Toliver. She's the one who spread the rumor about Ray and Evie getting a divorce. We got that straightened out and we had tea with the elderly lady. Her name is Rose. She's very sharp and she told us about her second husband's stamp collecting interests. I want you to explain about plate numbers. He had a specialized collection of British stamps exhibiting those markings."

"What was Ray doing, playing golf?"

"I didn't even see Ray. He was working on a lawn mower trying to figure out why it wouldn't start. He got it running about the time I started home."

"This Mrs. Toliver; she was married more than once?"

"Yes, three times. We invited her to attend one of our bridge club meetings—the one next Tuesday at Evie's. All she has to do is walk across the street, easy access. I think we'll be learning something from her. She used to be a good player."

"How old is she? Could she be suffering from dementia?"

"Not that Evie and I could determine. She was putting us on about hearing loss, but she was just teasing. We'll find out more about her wellbeing on Tuesday. All four of us will be observing her. Dotty used to work at an eldercare facility, her evaluation will be the one to rely on."

Frank nodded and turned away motioning me to follow him, "Come into my stamp room. I'll be your plate number coach. Then we'll have some lunch."

I had no idea stamps could be so interesting. Frank showed me several sheets of stamps from the United States and then I asked some questions. "But Mrs. Toliver said the early stamps of Great Britain were mostly one color. Why would her husband want to study them? Wouldn't that be boring?"

"Let me show you something interesting." Frank reached above his desk, pulled a book from the shelf, one of his stamp catalogs. He turned to Great Britain and pointed out where the plate numbers were on some of the early stamps. The plate number was on each stamp, not on the sheet selvage. He had one of the stamps, so he pulled out a magnifying glass and showed me where the plate number was in the scrollwork. I had no idea plate numbers on early stamps would be so fascinating. I began to realize why collectors could get so wound up with their bits of paper.

I had to comment, "That is intriguing, Frank. Thanks for the lesson." I started down the hall. "Let's have lunch. I'm in the mood for a toasted cheese sandwich and lemonade. What do you think?"

"I'll go for that. Do we have any grape jelly?"

"Yes, but we have to cut calories, so let's stay away from the jelly. Okay?"

Frank gave me a dirty look and sighed, "You're no fun, Marilee. I suppose you want me to taste the cheese. Cheese sandwiches are dry."

I giggled, "What do you think the lemonade is for?"

CHAPTER 5

Sunday was partly cloudy but by ten o'clock the sky had cleared. Church was at eleven and I wanted us to go, but Frank had other plans. His novel garage sale purchase was like a new baby, taking even more time than his collection. He was aligning a spotter scope, a new term to me, when I left for church. Evie was going to meet me there with Mrs. Toliver. They called about nine o'clock to see if I was going to hear the sermon.

After cleaning up the kitchen and putting clothes in the washer, I took a shower and spent the next half hour dressing and applying makeup. I left home at ten-forty headed to the Methodist church. Rose and Eve lived about ten minutes away, so that would give us plenty of time to gather at the church, only about a mile from the Meyers'. We shouldn't miss anything.

Following the services, we decided to take our time returning home. Mrs. Toliver had never been to The Olive Leaves restaurant, so Eve and I treated her to lunch. She wanted to pay her fair share, but we wouldn't allow it. Our conversation was so enjoyable, we didn't return to Evie's place until a little after two o'clock. I followed Evie and Rose to the Meyers' and went in with my friends to check out Evie's new furniture arrangement for Tuesday's bridge club gathering. Evie wanted Rose to see the arrangement so she wouldn't be uncomfortable when she joined our group. I was pleased to see what Evelyn had set up, a separate desk and chair for the fifth member when the other four were playing.

There was a note for Evie on the card table. She read it to us, "Frank and I are going hunting. Be back late, probably after dark."

"Is that my Frank?"

She shrugged her shoulders and said, "It just says Frank, probably Frank Antell from the bank. Does your husband like to hunt?"

"Not that I'm aware of. I can't remember him ever saying anything about hunting. He's probably at home fooling with that telescope. I think he's in love with the damn thing."

She smiled, "Ah, you're a little jealous."

I thought for a moment and replied, "I was at first, but I have a bridge group and Frank only has employees at the post office. It's not the same. I realized he needs other distractions from work, so it's okay that he has his stamps and telescope. He doesn't own a gun, so I think it's a little strange that he would be hunting. Maybe you're right, the Frank mentioned in the note is not my Frank."

I got home at three o'clock after spending nearly thirty minutes at Evie's. On the short drive, I wondered if Frank would be gone and a note like Evie found would be waiting. As I pulled into the driveway, Frank's car was in its usual place, so he's undoubtedly working on his stamps. That's his usual activity for Sunday afternoon. I wondered what he ate for lunch, maybe a peanut butter sandwich and hot chocolate.

The door to the kitchen was locked, so Frank must not be home. I searched my purse for the key, unlocked the door and expected Fred to be on the other side. I entered carefully to avoid stepping on the little four legged guy with the wagging tail, but surprise, no one greeted me, neither Fred nor Blemish. The house was alarmingly quiet.

I called out, "Fred? Blemish?" Then I heard a meow and Blemish approached from the living room. "Where's Fred?" Blemish didn't reply of course, so I went to the slider and looked out on the patio. Fred looked like he was sleeping on the cushioned rocking chair, but when I opened the sliding door he jumped to the ground and ran to me. He didn't bark but his tail was just a blur. I noticed Frank had filled Fred's water bowl before he left with Ray, at least that was my assumption. Frank had been thinking.

I carried out a brief survey of the backyard and then checked Frank's stamp room. No telescope. That's why he went with Ray, to focus his optics on distant objects, probably spotting animals for the guy with the gun. Then it occurred to me that Ray might be hunting with a bow, not a gun. I knew Ray took up archery a few years back after watching the Olympics. I guess I'll get all the details when Frank gets back. I think he'll be really enthusiastic about Ray including him on a hunting expedition.

I went into the living room and turned on the TV with the remote. That's when I saw Frank's note in the middle of the sofa. I sat down to read the chicken tracks. Frank should have been a doctor. His handwriting has always been terrible but I've learned how to decipher his hieroglyphics. If he had been in the military, I'm sure he would write in Morse Code.

Marilee: Ray and I have gone into the mountains to look for black bears. I'm going along to use my telescope to search for the animals. I doubt if we'll get a bear, but Ray wants one for a rug. He says the meat isn't good. I imagine we'll get back late, so don't wait up for me. P.S. I didn't feed Fred or Blemish— **. I had to smile at his asterisk kisses.

Ray and I drove on descending gravel and dirt roads for nearly an hour before turning off the main paths onto a Forest Service road. It led to a winding path that took us halfway to the bottom of a valley between Blue Ridge and Lost Ridge. Ray, during the previous week at the bank, checked out topographic maps and expected to find some bears at that location. His Internet searches found berries, a stream and plenty of cover, items on every bear's wish list.

I always wondered what bank executives did in those back rooms where no one could observe their activity. I thought Marilee would have opinions based on afternoon TV programs. But as far as I knew, Ray was a straight shooter and didn't get into any hanky-panky. Besides, I had seen the bank's secretaries and Evelyn had much more to offer.

Ray pulled over in a wide spot and we got out to take a look. I wished I had brought a camera; the picturesque valley was beautiful. The stream threaded through a copse of shrubs and young trees.

Ray motioned from the outer edge of the road, "Get your scope, Frank."

I followed his directions, lifted my scope from the back seat and extended the tripod's legs to full length. I planted the tripod firmly on the ground and focused on the stream. As I scoured the area for movement, I could hear Ray's breathing coming closer. He obviously wanted to get a better look.

I backed away and said, "Here, take a look. I didn't see anything. I bet the water is good to drink without any treatment. It looks ready for bottling from here. If we don't see any bears, we can do some fishing."

Ray obviously knew how to use a telescope, slewing the instrument side to side and changing the azimuth. He commented, "Nice scope, Frank, far better than my ten power rifle scope. Wide field of view also. What power is it?"

"Twenty with that eyepiece. I didn't bring any others." I didn't figure we would be counting pine needles on trees.

He backed away and I handed him his gun. With the gun in position to fire, he suddenly called out, "I see a bear!"

I quickly focused where he was pointing his gun and said, "Don't shoot, Ray. That's a momma with two cubs. That's illegal."

"Yeah, I know. She's too small anyway. Let's watch for a few minutes and then move on. There probably won't be any males nearby."

I crossed the road to the car and sat in the passenger seat looking at a map. According to the topographic representation, there was another similar site about a mile away. I took the map and showed Ray what appeared to be another good spot for bear detection. Our destination was on the same dirt road we had followed to discover the female and her cubs.

I loaded the telescope and Ray's gun in the back seat and we were off to the next spot. Ray glanced at me and queried, "Hungry?"

I nodded, "Yeah, hunting bears wears me out. I'm not used to so much hiking."

Ray laughed and said, "Eve made us some sandwiches and coffee's in the Thermos." He pointed behind his seat with his thumb. "See if you can reach the basket. If not, I'll pull over in a few minutes so we can chow down."

I tried to grab the wicker basket, but the seat head rests prevented my extended hand from contacting the container. I was at least half a foot from touching the picnic basket. I sat back and suggested, "Let's wait until we stop the car; I can't reach the basket."

"That's okay, we're halfway there. Five more minutes."

We made a sharp lefthand turn and Ray hit the brakes. I barely had a chance to resume my position in the passenger's seat and relatch my safety belt when we stopped suddenly. A small tree was lying across the road blocking our path.

Ray cut the engine and said, "Time to eat and evaluate."

We exited the vehicle and Ray extracted the basket from behind his seat. I was in front of the car checking out the tree blocking the road. I wondered if Ray had an axe, it wouldn't take much to cut the tree in half and drag the sections to the shoulder. One thing was certain, no one had been this way in the recent past. It appeared to me the shallow rooted tree had blown down during a recent storm.

As I evaluated the situation, I realized we were stymied and could go no farther. We would have to turn around and go to another site unless we could find another route to our second destination. Ray and I sat in the car with the doors open talking about our predicament while we ate sandwiches. I had expected the sandwiches to contain some esoteric seafood like sardines, but they were cheese and bologna or peanut butter and strawberry jelly.

"Well, I don't have an axe in my car, so I guess we'll have to retreat."

"Yeah, there's a hill on the left and a drop-off to the right. I do have another idea though."

"What's that?"

"We could start the tree on fire."

"That's crazy, Frank."

"But think about it. The forest service would come and put out the flames and remove the blockage. Then we could hunt for your rug." I looked at Ray and smiled.

He grinned and replied, "I don't believe a jail cell would have a bear skin rug."

"I wouldn't know, I've never been in jail or even visited one."

Ray remained quiet for a moment and said, "Let's have some coffee and turn the car around."

I didn't have to think about it, "Sounds like a good idea."

While we stimulated our heart burn, Ray came up with another idea. "Hand me that map, Frank." Ray unfolded the map and traced the road with his right forefinger to our present position. He then backtracked to the closest sideroad and followed that line to what I figured was a stream. I asked, "Have you found an alternate route?"

"Maybe. There's a road that leads to a stream but the map doesn't indicate a crossing—no bridge." He looked at me and said, "Let's take a look, perhaps the water isn't very deep."

"I'm game."

Not appreciating my humor, Ray gave me a scowl. "Let's turn around and take a look. I'd sure like to get a bear today. Are you with me?"

As if I had a choice, I replied, "We can try it. How far out of the way is this stream?"

"It looks like it's a component of the same water system that we saw part of before, where momma bear and the cubs were. About a mile from here and a little lower elevation. Maybe more berries and more bears."

We got back in the car, turned around and drove an estimated mile to the stream. I was worried about the clearance but Ray wanted to drive straight through the water. I told him we had better investigate the water's depth—if we got stuck there was no one to pull us out. We might have to walk miles for assistance. I was worried about Marilee wondering where I was if Ray and I started back home really late. And tomorrow was a workday.

Ray popped the trunk and put on waders. I gave him an old branch that would double as a probe or a walking stick in case the stream bed was slippery. The water didn't look deep but he had taken about eight steps and it was at least half a foot above his knees. It wasn't shallow enough to stay out of the passenger compartment, unless we drove through at high speed, risking a wreck.

I said, "Come on back Ray, let's go home. We can try another time. Besides, the bears will be bigger in another week. You'll have a larger rug." I smiled as I climbed into the car.

"Yeah, I guess you're right." Ray seldom agreed with me.

CHAPTER 6

Two and a half hours later, Ray dropped me off at my driveway. He asked me if I would like to go again next week, but on Saturday. I hesitated, not being excited about killing a bear, and said, "I'll have to ask Marilee if she has anything planned. I'll call on Wednesday if I don't see you sooner. Okay?"

Ray nodded and waved as he drove away. I hoped he was beginning to understand I didn't favor shooting a bear in order to make a rug from its hide. I watched his car stop at the end of the block, turn right and disappear behind neighbors' houses. I carried my telescope to the kitchen door and tried the knob. The door was locked. Rather than fish through my pockets for the key and place the scope on the ground, I knocked. Ten seconds later, the outside light came on as Marilee peered through the curtains. I saw a smile erupt from her face and watched the doorknob turn. When the door opened, she uttered, "Who's there?"

I laughed and replied, "The dishwasher repair man, I brought a telescope with me."

Marilee held the screen door open wide so I could get in with my scope. She stated, "I thought you would be coming home in the dark, the sun is just going down. Was Ray's bear hunt successful?"

I shook my head and replied, "Nah, but we saw a female and two cubs," as I placed my burden in the living room.

"Too cute to shoot?"

"Clever, Marilee. No, it's against the law." I noted the TV was on but I couldn't tell what program she was watching, a commercial for a pickup was on. I wondered how long a truck would last if the average owner drove like that. The pickup would probably spend most of the time in the shop being repaired.

I asked, "What did you have for dinner? Whatever it was, could you please warm it up? I'm going to take a shower and get into my pajamas."

Marilee replied, "Go take your shower. I'll warm up the casserole and get the salad from the fridge. I'll get you a bib so you don't get your jammies dirty."

I replied, "Thanks, Mom. I won't be long." I headed for the bedroom for my bedclothes and then the bathroom. I stopped for a moment to scrutinize the new addition to the hallway nook. I wondered how to retrieve the pennies we were going to use each morning because eventually, the inside of the scale would be full of pennies. At some point, if the money wasn't removed, it would probably foul the mechanism that does the weighing. I'll let Marilee know my concerns when we weigh in the morning.

Instead of showering, I decided to soak in the tub. Unless Marilee ran the dishwasher and the clothes washer simultaneously, there should be plenty of hot water. When the bath pond was about six inches deep, I slipped into the porcelain container and relaxed, something I hadn't done in a long time.

I don't know how long I had been soaking when a knock on the door occurred and Marilee looked in. I think I must have fallen asleep, 'cause she startled me. When I heard, "Frank, there's a shark in our bathtub!," I reached for a bar of soap and lathered in the appropriate places, pulled the plug and used the shower to rinse off. Marilee was still laughing when I returned to the kitchen. I don't know how she came up with that shark comment. I didn't comment but if the roles were reversed I think I would have used dolphin or baby whale.

I was in my pajamas and bathrobe when I sat down to eat. Marilee draped a kitchen towel, her substitute for a bib, across my chest and shoulders. I was pleased that she didn't drag out a baby's bib that our daughter used when she was a toddler. We talked about our activities of the day while I ate. I volunteered details of Ray's and my hunt and the reason we returned home earlier than expected.

Marilee had spent most of her day talking on the phone with Robin, our daughter, and the members of the bridge club. She informed Dorothy and Sheri of Evelyn's and her invitation for Mrs. Toliver to join the group on the following Tuesday. Sheri asked if Rose Toliver was going to be a permanent member of the group. Marilee told them the members would make that decision after the club meeting. Any judgment would have to be unanimous.

Monday morning was the initial weigh-in at the Neallys'. Before Marilee went to bed, she pinned a calendar to the nook wall above the scale with a ballpoint resting on the top of the scale's white enamel surface. Marilee was up first, visited the bathroom and upon exiting, stepped on the scale and dropped a penny in the slot. When she saw the result, she had to decide to lie or record her actual weight. She wrote down 149 followed with a pound sign and shook her head a little dismayed; she had to lose weight or face medical problems; she wasn't getting any younger. Her doctor had warned her of diabetes and heart disease. She was about thirty pounds overweight. Frank was afraid of what his doctor would tell him.

Marilee returned to the bedroom and got dressed as Frank stirred and took his journey to the porcelain palace. When he left the bathroom, she heard the sounds of a penny dropping and movements of the scale mechanism as the pointer swung through the numbers. She heard, "Humm, that's not good." She wasn't going to ask about the number, she would wait for Frank to divulge his weight or she would find out later what he had recorded. She wondered what Frank would think of their new plan to shed excess baggage. However, there wasn't going to be encouragement of his reaction, it was too soon. Maybe after a week or two Frank will volunteer something: no pressure.

Little time was spent on breakfast, Frank and Marilee both reflecting on the numbers from the scale. Frank had a piece of toast, a small glass of orange juice, a cup of coffee, gave Marilee a kiss and was off to the post office. Marilee hadn't counted on her husband's sullen behavior; he hadn't even inquired about what she had planned for the day. That was not usual but not so unusual either. Sometimes when he had a pressing task in mind he would not say a word. Marilee sat at the table with her coffee for a few minutes before hearing a car in the driveway.

Before I was on my feet at the door to see who had arrived, Frank suddenly entered the kitchen. "I'm back! I forgot my wallet, it's in my other pants."

"Oh, I'll get it. Have the rest of my coffee."

His bear hunting pants were folded and stuffed in the hamper for dark clothes, the first place I looked. I hustled back into the kitchen and stuffed his billfold in his left rear pocket. I let him fasten the button.

He turned for the door saying, "Thanks, dear, and remember to get those pennies from the bank, we're gonna need a bunch."

"Don't worry, that's the only errand I have for the day. I'm going to study my bridge bidding book. I've got to be prepared for tomorrow."

As he hesitated before getting back in the car, he said, "Well, don't waste time playing solitaire." I could hear a chuckle as he slammed the car door.

I shook my head and smiled, closed the screen door and locked it. Frank warned me about several break-ins in town. We decided against buying a gun, but I kept the doors locked and carried my home phone with me at all times, even when going in the bathroom. Thank God for Wi-Fi. I poured another cup of coffee and sat down at the kitchen table with Thurston Ander's book, *How to Win at Bridge.* I figured I could read for an hour before dressing into something better to wear to the bank.

The bank opened at ten, so at nine forty-five, I put down my book and scooped up the deck of cards. I always dealt out cards to duplicate the hands shown in the illustrations. Going through the motions of playing the cards fixed the explanations in my mind.

Five blocks from the post office, the bank, encased in shiny black marble, was the central architectural feature of the town. Bullet proof glass and security cameras made customers and personnel feel safe at all times. A camera snapped a picture as a patron entered through the automatic doors. I arrived at ten after ten and walked to the nearest unoccupied teller. He greeted me with a smile and a pleasant, "Good morning, how may I help you?"

The young man appeared to be just out of high school, but for all I knew, he was a college graduate. His name tag said Lyle. These kids look so young.

I answered, "I'd like to get four rolls of pennies."

"Checking or savings?"

"No, I'll pay cash." I flipped open my purse, found my wallet and gave the teller two paper dollars.

"One moment please." Lyle smiled, turned away and walked quickly behind a partition. He was gone for about fifteen seconds and reappeared with four rolls of pennies. In one smooth motion he slid the rolls under the glass shield so I could pick them up. I dropped them in my purse and said, "Thank you, Lyle."

"You're welcome. Is there anything else I can help you with?"

I looked him in the eyes and said, "No, that's all I wanted." I thought he was giving me a funny grin but his eyes were focused over my head and behind me. I turned to see who it might be. The man was tall and I had to look up to see who was wearing the suit.

"Hello, Marilee. I thought it was you I saw on the security camera. What are you getting all those pennies for? Are you and Frank playing penny-ante poker?"

"Oh, hi Ray. No, Frank and I play strip poker. The pennies are for something else."

There was another person in line behind Ray and me so we stepped aside. Ray was chuckling about my comment. He didn't need to know what the coins were for. Besides, Evelyn would tell him after I inform the bridge club about Frank and me working on our slim-down plan.

"I assume Frank told you about our unsuccessful bear hunt. I hope he'll go with me on Saturday. He's got a much better telescope than I have on my rifle."

I felt like telling him Frank wasn't a fan of killing a bear to make the hide into a rug but decided to keep it to myself. I didn't have any thoughts for continuing the conversation, so I said, "I'd better get back home and you'd better go back to work. Don't you have some money to count?" I grinned. "Bye, Ray."

"Bye, Marilee. Tell Frank to be sure to call me in Wednesday."

"I'll do that, but I'm sure he will remember."

I walked toward the door and turned to see if Ray was watching me as I edged out the entranceway. I quickly scanned the lobby but Ray was gone. I wondered how often he came out of his office to chat with bank customers. Maybe he just wanted me to remind Frank to contact him on Wednesday.

By ten thirty, the sun was warming the storefronts and concrete. Both pedestrian and street traffic had increased dramatically during my short stay inside the bank. It was still cool inside the car, so I flicked the heater on the lowest setting. As I turned the key, a thought came to me. I'll drop by the antique store and ask Todd how to open the scale to retrieve the pennies. There was no hole for a key, so there must be a simple procedure for opening the panel to access the coin receptacle.

It took about five minutes to reach the antique shop after getting off Main. I turned off the heater, parked diagonally and entered the store. Todd addressed me immediately, "Hello, Mrs. Neally. How's that scale working for you?"

I was surprised he remembered my name but I smiled and replied, "It's fine but I have a question for you."

His eyebrows raised and he cocked his head a bit to the left. "Are you looking for something else?"

"No. How do I open the panel on the rear of the scale to retrieve the pennies?"

"That's a good question and I'm sorry to say I really don't know. That scale has been around for at least sixty or seventy years, perhaps even longer, according to the previous owner. I have never seen any operating directions. Maybe you can do a search on the Internet and find your answer. By chance, do you know anyone that might have been around long ago?"

I didn't have to think more than a second, "Yes, I do have an elderly friend." I knew I'd be seeing Rose Toliver tomorrow. I'll bug her.

CHAPTER 7

As I hastened home, I tried to keep my mind on driving but I kept thinking about asking Rose if she knew anything about our antique scale. The trip was quick and uneventful until I approached the driveway. There was a fancy yellow sports car parked in front of our mailbox. Unless the driver was hiding in the trunk, the car looked empty. I nearly stopped behind the strange car and copied the rear license plate. It was from Colorado and appeared valid. The date stickers were correct.

I didn't want to get out to walk around this unfamiliar vehicle, I liked the security my car interior offered. I decided to go around the block, reverse direction and check out the front plate. It must have taken about five minutes before I returned but the vehicle had vanished. Relieved the perceived threat was gone, I turned into my driveway and parked in my normal location leaving space for Frank to park next to the kitchen door.

Fred and Blemish were not interested in what I was doing, it wasn't time for their dinner. Blemish was on the back of the sofa looking out the picture window, I assumed looking for the mail carrier or watching for other animals. Fred was sitting on the floor beside the slider waiting for me to let him out. I had been inside the house for less than ten minutes when the phone rang. I had just placed it on the dining room table.

"Hello."

"Hi Marilee."

"Oh, hi Frances." It was my next-door neighbor.

"The woman that was driving that fancy yellow car was in your backyard. Do you know her?"

"It was a woman?"

"Yeah, maybe mid-twenties, short skirt, nice looking. She seemed to be in a hurry. She checked out your slider, peered in the glass. I heard your dog barking."

"Did you happen to get a picture of her?"

"Sorry, Marilee. By the time I got my phone, she was gone. I heard the roar of her engine and rushed to look out at her car but it had disappeared."

"Well, don't worry about it. I got her license number. Thanks for letting me know what she was doing."

"No problem, bye Marilee."

"Bye Fran."

My phone indicated eleven twenty. Time to get something started for lunch. I had some low salt, packed in water tuna and a quart jar of low-cal salad dressing, so I decided to make some tuna fish sandwiches and a salad with lettuce, carrots, radishes and cheese strips. Frank should like my concoction. I was ready for him at eleven fifty, so I sat and watched the end of an old TV western. The show concluded and went to commercial. I started to get up from the recliner when my phone chimed.

It was Frank. The sudden appearance of a postal rep from Denver required him to take the guy to lunch. He was sorry to miss our time at home but he'd tell me all about the meeting at dinner. What could I say? I thanked him for calling. I wondered what was that important, but then I got an idea. Perhaps Frank was getting a raise or a promotion. I had to think positively.

I enjoyed my lunch, cleaned up what little mess I had created and sat down with my book in preparation for tomorrow's bridge club meeting. I was in the middle of chapter two and woke up at three o'clock salivating on my blouse. That was a first for me, Frank was the one usually drooling after dinner when he fell asleep watching TV. I was always amused when he woke with a start and tried to conceal the wet spot on his shirt. Then, he usually retired to his stamp room to work on his collection before getting ready for the late news and bed.

When Frank attended his collection, I cleaned up the kitchen, placed dirty dishes in the washer and fed the animals. After completing kitchen activities, I resumed reading, most of the time a fictional story or a magazine article in the most recent copy of Ladies' New Literature Journal, a bimonthly.

Frank arrived home a few minutes after six and I told him about the female visitor. His reaction to our neighbor's sighting was surprisingly simple. "Sounds like some chick was looking for a boyfriend, trying to catch him cheating but went to the wrong address."

That had never occurred to me and seemed a reasonable explanation for what had taken place, so I dropped the subject. Before he even had a chance to tell me about his bank visitor, I recounted my visit to the antique shop. He wasn't surprised that Todd didn't know how to open the panel on the scale.

"Marilee, I think there must be a simple solution, but it isn't obvious. Let's not worry about it until we run out of pennies or foul up the mechanism. If we haven't figured it out by then, I'll get out my tools and attack the problem. I guarantee I'll get that damn panel off." He then removed his tie and went in the bedroom to change clothes. I got the idea he didn't want to discuss the small access door.

I almost followed him into the bedroom, but hesitated, thinking he would tell me about his lunchtime meeting during dinner. When he got out of his suit and into civvies his mood invariable improved. He'll probably go to the fridge and expect to get a beer. He won't find any. I didn't get booze of any kind at the market since it wasn't part of our new more wholesome diet. I had a strong feeling we were going to have an interesting evening meal.

As we began to eat, Frank asked me, "Would you like to hear what the bank rep wanted to speak to me about?"

I thought he was going to ask about the salad, it had been refrigerated since lunchtime, but still looked reasonably fresh, maybe not as perky as it might have been. I asked, "What was this gentleman's name, was it anyone I might have heard of?"

"Well, that's irrelevant, dear. It's what he asked me. Anyway, his name is Harrison Abrams. He's a vice president from the Denver office." Frank took a bite of salad, chewed, swallowed and continued, "He offered me the head position in the Boise office." He took another bite and grinned. "This is a good salad, why haven't we had this before?"

I had never heard of Harrison Abrams. I was trying to grasp what he had said about the job in Boise. "The salad was left over from lunch." I watched as he filled his mouth. "What did you tell Mr. Abrams?"

"I told him I couldn't take a job in another city without talking it over with my wife. He said he had to know right away, but he'd give me until tomorrow. So, what do you think?"

"You're retiring in two years, dear. How long would he want you to stay on in Boise?"

"A minimum of five years. My retirement would be greatly enhanced with the upgrade in salary. He made it sound like a good deal, but I don't want to work until I'm sixty-eight. I'd like to enjoy a few more years without any pressure."

"Couldn't you give notice after two years and just quit?"

"No, I would lose any earnings above what I'm making now. Besides, you know how much I enjoy hunting for bear with Ray." He grimaced and we laughed.

"Yes, and I would really miss the girls in my bridge club. Oh, we'd have to sell the house, find a new place in Boise and get a new phone number and car licenses. I wonder who our new neighbors would be?"

We sat there looking at each other for a moment and then he said, "I don't think the seeing is incredibly good in Boise. The city lights would force me to take a trip out of town to use my scope. I'm going to tell him I'm not interested. The increase in salary is good but being tied down for five years is a real killer. What do you think?"

"I'm all for staying put. I kinda like things the way they are. With my retirement and yours kicking in in a few years, we should be in fine shape for the future."

"I think you're right, but I worry about inflation and the mounting national debt. Our retirement might not be worth very much if spending in Washington, D.C. continues unabated. I wish we had more to say about that."

"I'm still worried about that sports car being in front of our house. I wonder what that woman was looking for. Can we have the police check her license number?"

Frank thought for a moment and replied, "Let's see if we can check on a plate number from our computer. If it works, I believe we can get the registered owner. We won't need the police then. Let's try it."

I followed Frank into his stamp room where we kept our computer. He pulled back the chair and motioned for me to sit. "You do the typing, you're better at it than I am, plus you know the license number." I reached under the table and flipped on the power switch. We waited a few seconds and I signed in with our code. I clicked on the browser, entered license number ID and we waited for a split second. I clicked on the first item and typed in the personalized plate, "TUF STUF."

I thought we would have to enter the state, but a listing popped up quickly, Sam Walker, Denver, Colorado. I looked at Frank and remarked, "I wonder if that is Samuel or Samantha?"

"Probably Samantha. Didn't Frances say she saw a young woman checking out our house?"

"Uh-huh, but she could have been driving her boyfriend's or her husband's car."

"I'd guess it was her car because of that license. Frances said the woman was sexy, didn't she?"

"Frances didn't say sexy, she said nice looking and she wore a short skirt."

"Yeah, sexy." He grinned.

"I'll see if I can contact her and have her meet you for coffee."

"You could do that, but I doubt if she would like to hear about my stamp collection. She's probably younger than our daughter." He chuckled.

"You could tell her all about your new telescope."

"Oh, I'll bet she would be real interested in that. But I could tell her about the valuable antique we have. She'd be impressed with the scale and all those pennies; thoughts of being rich."

I guess we both decided we had enough frivolousness. Frank opened one of his albums and I went to the kitchen to make a couple dozen cookies for tomorrow's club meeting. I finished the cookies at ten thirty. I heard Frank turn off the lights and leave his collection room, so I called to him, "Come have a cookie. I want to try them out on someone so none of my friends suffer."

Frank laughed and joined me in the kitchen. I warmed up the remains of our dinner coffee and we sat at the table snacking on cookies, one each. We had to weigh ourselves in the morning.

CHAPTER 8

Frank and I awoke to a rainy day but the weather report suggested a warm breeze would arrive at noon, clouds lifting and sun beams warming the town. I expected to see water vapor rising like smoke from our neighbor's roof by noon.

We started the second day of our weigh-ins using the first two cents of the pennies I had picked up at the bank Monday. When Frank joined me for breakfast, there was silence as he buttered his toast. I gave him a questioning look and he smiled back, "Two pounds lighter today, your plan seems to be working."

"Our plan, dear. I had no change from yesterday."

"Same everything?"

"Uh-huh. Maybe my metabolism hasn't had a chance to cope with the new diet yet."

"I hate to suggest this, but was it because of the cookies?"

"No, I didn't cheat. I had one small cookie and that was all. Actually, I gave you a bigger one."

Frank grinned, "Trying to sabotage my weigh-in, huh?"

I chuckled, "No, all the cookies were about the same size, except one. There was a little one when I was running out of dough. I confess, I licked the spoon that I used to transfer the dough to the cookie sheet. But that was only a tiny portion. My weight gain must have been water."

"Your bridge club meeting is today, right? You can't avoid calories when you're with those other gals. I don't expect you to starve yourself. Do Ray and Eve have an exercise machine?"

I chortled, "You want me to work off anything I eat at our club meeting?"

"No, I'm curious. Evelyn looks like she is in fairly good shape. Is she regularly active?"

I thought for a moment. "She plays tennis and rides one of those fixed cycles twice a week."

"Maybe we should start taking Fred for a walk after dinner. He probably would benefit from some exercise, don't you think?"

I nodded, "Yeah, licking two stamps with one wet tongue."

Frank grinned, finished the rest of his coffee and last bite of toast, pushed away from the table and said, "I think it will take us at least a week before we see any tangible results of our weighing. I've got to get to the office and meet with Abrams. He'll just have to look for another guy. Maybe he can find a woman to take the job. There are lots of qualified women working in the postal service."

"I wonder if he's ever thought of that. Maybe you should light a fire under him, stir the pot."

"I think I'll do that." He slipped into his blazer and overcoat, checked for his wallet and headed out the door, then stopped and turned around. "Come here."

I walked over to him and he gave me a kiss. "Good luck at your bridge club. Don't bring back any of those cookies, they're too good."

I watched him unlock and climb in the car, turn on the windshield wipers, back out of the driveway and disappear down the street. I stood in the doorway surveying the chilly neighborhood for a few seconds, stepped back inside and locked the door. As soon as I clean up the breakfast dishes, I'll take a shower and start getting ready to play bridge at Evie's. I have to remember to ask Mrs. Toliver about opening the access door on the scale to remove the pennies. I hope she knows the trick to removing the panel.

* * *

I was ready to set off to Evie's at one o'clock but decided to wait for half an hour. I'd get there in ten minutes, so I sat down with my bridge book and read for half an hour. I played a few hands, cards face up, as instructed, digested the author's analysis and checked my watch. Time to go. I'd arrive a little early, but I could help Evie set up for the meeting. Starting out the kitchen door, I almost forgot the cookies. I went back inside, grabbed the Tupperware container and resumed leaving the house. Frank would probably make me throw them out if I had left them in the kitchen. He's really serious about us losing weight. I didn't realize he would be so earnest when I proposed our new regimen. He even suggested more exercise by walking Fred.

I was the second member of our group to arrive at Meyers'. Dotty Higgin's fire truck was parked at the curb blocking the mailbox. I had to smile when I saw that big vehicle. I'll forever think she drives a fire truck, even though it's just a big red suburban. I bet it's a real gas hog. How can they stand to pay to fill the tank? I got out of my car with the container of cookies, locked the doors and strode to Meyers' entrance. I was met by Dotty who informed me, "Evie's in the kitchen, come on in. I'll take your jacket."

"Thanks, Dotty, just put it on the back of one of the chairs." I handed her the Tupperware container. "Give these to Evie, freshly made last night."

"Did Frank assist you?"

I had to grin, "You're kidding, he just pays the bills." I happened to look out the front picture window and saw Rose Toliver exiting her front door. It struck me that she might need help coming across the street, so I slipped into my jacket and went back outside. She had only taken about ten steps by the time I crossed the street; she was watching where she was placing her feet. Although she hadn't mentioned her equilibrium was not particularly good, I suspected she was wary of falling. I didn't want to startle her, so I waited at the curb when she would look up.

"Hi, Rose, are you ready to play some bridge?"

"Well, I am if I can get across the street. Are you my escort?" She studied my face and said, "You are Marilee, aren't you?"

"That's correct. Before we cross the street, I have a question for you. I hope you can help me."

"You're going to ask if I remember to look both ways?"

I couldn't refrain from laughing. "No, that's not it. I bought an antique scale last week and there is a panel on the back but there is no access using a key. I wonder if you know how to open it."

Rose looked at me crazily, almost shocked. Then she said, "You'll have to describe the scale. I just might know how to access the inside of the unit. It's been a long time since I worked in a store that had one of those old retail merchandizing machines. The ones used these days are quite different." She looked at Meyers' house and said, "Let's get going, we don't want to be late."

We started across the street and heard a car coming. We both glanced at it and Rose said, "I hope the driver sees us."

I recognized the car, it was Sheri Sandborne in her light-green Subaru Outback. I commented, "That's another of our bridge club members, she won't hit us. If she did, there wouldn't be a foursome."

Rose nodded. "Well, maybe we'd have a foursome at the hospital."

We both chuckled as we started across the grass toward Meyers' front door. Sheri had parked her SUV and was closing fast behind us. I had never seen her move so fast.

She called out, "Hey ladies, wait for me!"

I still had my hand about shoulder high on the door after ushering Rose inside when Sheri ducked under my arm and entered the foyer. I shut the door, locked it and said, "Sheri, I'd like you to meet Rose Toliver. She's going to join our group today. Rose lives across the street. We'll rotate her in and out as we proceed. Rose is an experienced player. I wouldn't be surprised if we all learn something from her."

After we talked with Rose for a few minutes, she said, "I'll watch a few hands and get used to your bidding, and since I'm old enough to be your mother, I don't want you to call me anything but Rose, especially not Mrs. Toliver."

We smiled and Evie said, "As you all can see, I've put two card tables together at their corners. I'll sit at one position and we'll draw cards for the rest of the positions. High card sits to my left and so forth. The refreshments, tea, coffee, and Marilee's cookies will be at the other table and Rose will sit there temporarily."

Evie sat down, extracted a new deck of cards from her purse, peeled off the cellophane wrapping, removed the jokers and advertising, and shuffled. We all drew a card. I got the high card, the ace of spades, so sat at Evie's left, Sheri sat opposite Evie, so was her partner and Dotty became my ally. After evaluating my cards, I bid two clubs, Shari passed, Dotty bid three no trump and Evie passed. Three no trump was made easily. We actually made one over.

Rose sat by quietly, biting her lower lip, but as I watched her closely, I could tell by her facial contortions she didn't approve of our bidding. After a half hour, we had refreshments and as I sipped some tea and looked at our scores, all of us were playing very conservatively.

Rose was keeping her thoughts to herself, but before long I could tell she was going to explode. I felt she was itching to get in the game.

Dotty whispered to me, "I've been watching Rose. I'll sit out the next hand so she can play. I'll go to the bathroom for a while. I'll take something to read." She looked through some of Evie's magazines, picked up one on home designs and announced, "Rose will take my place, I'm going to do some reading in the bathroom." She smiled, "It might take some time." We all grinned and laughed at her suggestion of constipation; she had always complained about just the opposite. She had even seen a doctor about it.

It was Dotty's turn to deal, so Rose accepted the duty. Her dexterity with the deck reminded me of a magician doing card tricks. She glanced at all of us and remarked, "I've been practicing at home, it has been a long time since I last played bridge. My hands are a bit stiff."

Rose arranged her cards with a few deft motions and she waited for the rest of us to evaluate ours. I bid one heart, Sheri passed and Rose said, "Four no trump." I looked at her in amazement and she smiled, "We've got this." With a determined look, Evie doubled. I laid out the dummy hand and Evie led the first card. Rose gobbled up the first trick and in a short time she took nine more, giving up the last three to a king, a queen and a jack, all in different suits.

Sheri kept score and remarked, "If Evie hadn't doubled, I would have. That was amazing, Rose."

I reacted, "I think I have a lot to learn about bidding. I would have settled for three no trump."

"Well, I had one long suit and I gambled that we had another, so ten tricks seemed to be a pretty safe contract. I should have redoubled, darn it."

As I gathered the cards for Evie, Rose asked a question. "How big is that scale and what color is it, Marilee?"

Before I had a chance to answer, she added, "And what is the heaviest weight it will register?"

Just before Evie dealt the cards, I hesitated, then said, "I guess it's about four feet high and is white. Were they made in other colors?"

"Well, most were white, but I've seen some in brown and one in red. Most of the white ones were in pharmacies or department stores, as I recall. Some of the other colors were in shoe stores and toy stores. Scales might have been repainted by merchants."

Evie began dealing the cards and I thought to myself, Why would Rose want so much information? All I wanted was to figure out how to open the back panel to remove the pennies. I remembered she asked the maximum that could be weighed. "It goes up to 350 pounds. When Frank was on the scale I stepped on for a moment and it went up to 350."

Rose nodded, "Interesting."

We continued playing for another hour before Rose sighed and said, "I think I've had enough for today. I need to rest awhile before I have dinner." She got up, pushed her chair back and thanked us for letting her join our group. We stood and thanked her for her interesting contribution to our afternoon. Then she asked, "I don't want to overdue my welcome, but could I join you again next week?"

We surveyed each other and all nodded. Evie said, "Sure, Rose. We enjoyed having you take part. Our next meeting will be at Marilee's house. You can ride with me. Marilee likes us to meet at one o'clock instead of two."

Rose responded, "Oh, that will be fine. I'll come over here at twelve forty-five. Is that okay?"

"Sure. That will be fine. It's only a short drive."

Evie accompanied Rose to the door and offered to go across the street with her, but she refused and strode away as if she were much younger than when I accompanied her across the street earlier. We all watched Rose navigate from Evie's driveway across the asphalt to her own concrete, slowing her pace after she reached her property. It was my opinion Rose knew we were watching her return home. I was impressed with her knowledge and play at our meeting. I think we all were.

We played one more hand before preparing to disperse for our homes. Evie reminded, "Next week we'll be at Marilee's. Remember to come an hour earlier than today." She grinned, "We'll either play longer or quit earlier." We all laughed at her announcement. Then she added, "I'll ferry Rose. Sheri, you bring some sweets, maybe some low-cal stuff."

I added, "I'll have something to drink. Any requests?"

Dotty grinned, "How about some wine? Not the cheap kind, either."

She knew what I would say and she looked at me expecting me to downplay her suggestion. I said, "It will have to be the cheap stuff, if I get any. Frank and I are on a budget, not just a new diet."

Dotty turned serious, "I was just joking, Mari. You always have the best coffee."

Sheri chimed in, "That's right."

As I drove home, I kept thinking about Rose's curious interest in my recently acquired antique, but maybe I was imagining something. Perhaps she was just intrigued with my old device. I'll find out next week.

CHAPTER 9

It seemed like the only topic that generated a conversation between Frank and me during the week was his phone call to Raymond. Of course, we both had our own doings, my reading the book about bridge and Frank working on his collection and garage sale telescope. Wednesday evening, he called Ray and to my great surprise, Frank agreed to go bear hunting on Saturday.

Following the phone call, which I couldn't help overhearing, I commented, "I thought you didn't want to help Ray kill a bear, just to make a rug from the hide. I can't understand killing an animal to make a rug."

Frank sat on the sofa in silence for several seconds before responding. I knew he had to hold off snapping at me. He smiled and replied, "I'm not going to help him, I'm going to help protect the bear."

"And how will you accomplish that?"

"I'll make noises, give him the wrong distances and wind velocity and generally make a nuisance of myself."

"So, you're going to risk pissing him off?"

"Yeah, but I don't want him to get too riled and shoot me. I want to discourage him from asking me to go hunting with him again."

"You could have turned him down for this Saturday."

"That's true, but he would probably ask me to go another time."

"You think it will sabotage playing golf with him?"

"No, he wants me to play golf against him. He knows he's a little better than I am. He likes to win when the outcome is in his favor. He's kind of like a little kid. I just enjoy the competition, plus we usually have a beer afterward. Unfortunately, the loser pays. I've paid for a lot of beers in the last few years."

"So, you're always losing?"

"Not always, just most of the time. We don't bet, but I always take at least ten bucks to pay for the beer. I'm getting better though, and if losing weight improves my game, he'll start forking over for the beer before long."

"But then he'll look for another golf buddy."

"If he does, I'll spend more time with my collection and I've been thinking about getting a camera to take some pictures using the telescope."

"Of the neighbors?" I smiled.

He laughed, "No, stars and planets. Jupiter and Saturn make great subjects for astronomers with cameras. I might have to buy a bigger scope, a twelve inch reflector, or something even bigger."

"And where are you going to get the money to pay for it?"

"I'll sell off some of my collection. It's worth quite a bit of money now."

"You never told me much about its value. Is it insured?"

"You bet it is, for about fifty thousand dollars. It's probably underinsured, I haven't kept up with the trend in values in the last five years or so. I should update things this year. I'll have more time after I get Ray off my neck about bear hunting. I can use Saturdays to catalog my collection."

"I'd like to go somewhere and do something different. When the snow comes, we're landlocked. What about buying snowshoes or getting some skis? After we lose some weight, we can do more exercising, can't we?"

I looked at Frank and noticed his eyes were closed and he was breathing slowly and shallowly. He must be asleep. I said, "Frank, what do you think?"

He didn't answer for about ten seconds. Just as I was about to shake him, he answered, "Sure, we can get snowboards, ice skates, skis, anything you want. I'm getting tired, dear, let's get in bed. Bring that book about bridge and read to me. That'll put me to sleep."

"You could read one of your stamp catalogs. That will put us both to sleep."

"Yeah, but I like to drift off with the sound of your sexy voice."

I started laughing and Frank couldn't help adding his baritone giggle. When we were in bed, we both fell asleep in about ten minutes. I woke up at 1:30, put my book on the floor and turned off the reading light. Fred was curled up on the bed at our feet.

Friday evening, Frank and I went to Roscoe's Sporting Goods and checked out the winter gear. We didn't spend a cent, but we had fun looking and checking out the costs. I recorded prices of some of the items we thought might serve our needs. After getting back home we decided to get boots, jackets and snowshoes for ourselves and corresponding winter wear for Fred. We didn't think Blemish would want to go out in the deep snow except in our backyard and that was only occasionally. Last year it was evident she didn't like the snow or the accompanying low temperatures. When our estimate of the total bill started to exceed four hundred dollars, we began to question the whole idea.

Frank suggested, "What if we buy boots this month, jackets next month and wait for the first big snowfall before we get snowshoes?"

I had to agree. There was no immediate reason to make our credit card payment balloon nearly out of control. That two percent back from the bank was not going to amount to much. As we got ready for bed, I inspected my winter puffy coat. It was still in good condition and therefore it was unnecessary to buy a new winter coat to be used for our cold season activities, savings: over a hundred dollars. However, Frank didn't have a winter coat aside from his suitcoat which was inappropriate for traipsing through snow. It was a good windbreak, but that was about all.

After a short discussion, he sided with me, especially since it would lessen the severity of a deep depression in our bank account. He asked, "Is there anything else you can think of?"

"Nope! But I'll think about it. Maybe by morning I'll come up with something."

Frank extinguished the reading light and said, "Good night babe."

I pulled the covers around my neck, sighed and replied, "Night, Frank."

I opened my right eye and saw Frank adjusting the blinds. He had on a sweatshirt and underpants. It was five-thirty. My left eye was buried in my pillow. At first I thought I might be dreaming but then I heard him say, "Damn, it's snowing!"

"How can you tell, it's dark outside."

"Oh, sorry I woke you. I couldn't sleep so I thought I'd get up and check the weather. Tiny flakes are drifting past the streetlight.

It's just going to be a dusting, not enough to halt a bear hunt. I'll build a fire so the living room will be warm when you get up. I won't start the furnace."

I mumbled, "Thank you dear," and went back to sleep.

I heard a car door slam but didn't open my eyes. The clock display was seven thirty-five when the phone rang. "Hello?" No one spoke so I hung up and decided to get out of bed and start my day. The log in the fireplace was almost gone but there were still some glowing coals remaining. I tossed on a couple of pieces of kindling, added some wadded scrap paper and watched smoke rise for about a minute before a flame appeared and spread the length of the kindling which told me to add another log.

I had watched Frank tend the fire numerous times but had never started one myself. I wrestled a small log on top of the flames. As the log caught fire and sporadic crackling started, I wanted to pat my back for a job well done. I felt naïve for not knowing about taking care of fireplace fires. We had gone on barbeques before but someone else always took care of the fires. I didn't pay but slight attention.

Fred and Blemish greeted me when I walked into the kitchen. Ha, I guess I imagined the greeting, they barely looked up from their water bowls. Fred left to continue his night's sleep and Blemish climbed on the back of the sofa and looked out the front window at the sparkling slightly white sidewalk. The snow was like Frank had said, just a thin layer of the white stuff. The grass was still green. We usually had several of these occurrences before we got a real winter snowfall of several inches to more than a foot.

I noticed Frank had fried some eggs and the toaster was pulled away from the backsplash. Evidently, from the crumbs, it looked like he made two slices of toast. He hadn't made any coffee. Then I noticed a glass in the sink with remnants of orange juice. I had made a couple of sandwiches for him and the paper bag was gone from the fridge. I assumed Ray would have a well-stocked picnic basket in his car for the hunt. I toasted a piece of whole-wheat bread, boiled water for tea and started Mr. Coffee to make six cups of high test for the rest of the day.

I was ready to read by nine o'clock and was headed for the sofa when I remembered carrying my book in the bedroom last night. I turned and started down the hallway. When I saw the scale, I realized I forgot to weigh myself this morning. I checked the calendar to see if Frank remembered. He hadn't or forgot to record his weight. I'll have to make sure we use the scale tomorrow morning. I'll put a little sticky note on my slippers.

Mr. Coffee beeped announcing the brew was ready, so I poured a holiday mug full, grabbed my book and joined Blemish on the sofa. I'll have reheated tea later. The next chapter was on finessing and I began to read. I had only gotten to the second page of the chapter when the doorbell rang. All I could think of was one of those roofing or siding salesman was going to tell me his company would be in the neighborhood and he wanted to warn me about the noise. That kind of noise doesn't bother me in the least but Fred and Blemish might not like it.

I flipped back the Afghan, marked my place, put my nearly full mug on the coffee table and went to see who had rung the bell. I kind of hoped whoever it was had decided to leave since I took so long to come to the door. I was mildly shocked when I swung the door open. Rose Toliver was standing there with a whimsical smile. She wore a long gray coat and a blue scarf was wrapped tightly around her neck. Nothing covered her tousled gray hair.

"Rose! How did you get here?" I glanced around for a car but the street was empty. "Come in, it's cold out this morning."

She moved into the house rather quickly for an elderly woman, and said, "I walked. I looked up your address and decided to come see that scale. I'm very curious, you know."

"I'll show it to you after you get warmed up, okay?"

"Well, all right. I hope I'm not bothering you and your husband."

"You're no bother. Frank isn't home. He's out with Ray Meyers trying to shoot a bear. Ray wants a bearskin rug."

"He should go to Alaska for his bear. They are much larger up there. Say, do you have some young neighbors that have a sports car? I saw a gaudy yellow one about a block from here. It was parked at the curb."

"Did you notice the license plate?"

"I did. Only because I thought it was stupid." She spelled, "T-U-F S-T-U-F."

I nodded, realizing that was the same car I had seen parked in front of my house several days ago. "I've seen that car, Rose. It is very fancy. It was parked out in front at the curb, a yellow sports model. Did you see the driver?"

"No, but the driver and passenger couldn't be far away. There wasn't any top. They'll freeze their rear ends in this weather."

"There were two people, not just a woman?"

"Oh, I couldn't tell but both seats were devoid of clutter, no junk and no snow." She was trying to warm her hands by rubbing them together.

"Can I get you a cup of coffee?"

She thought for a moment and replied, "Yes, that would be nice. I'm allowed one cup a day—caffeine affects my blood pressure and pulse. I used to drink coffee all day long, but that's in the distant past now. We used to pay a nickel a cup at the city library."

"Here in town?"

She chuckled, "Oh, no. That was in Omaha—back in the 70s. Gosh, that was fifty years ago."

We gabbed and sipped coffee for fifteen minutes before Rose suddenly stood, smoothed her pants and asked, "Where is that scale, Marilee? I want to take a look."

I rose from the sofa and said, "Follow me, it's down the hall outside the bathroom." We were only a few steps away from the item of interest. I flipped on the hall light and waved my hand at the scale like a model does on a TV quiz show when indicating the winner's prize.

Rose came closer to inspect the white enameled antique, reached out and rubbed the small dent in the finish at the top left side. She sighed and requested, "Do you have a nickel?"

"It uses pennies for weighing. They're in a little tray on that knickknack shelf at the right."

"I don't need a penny, Marilee, I want a nickel. I'm not going to weigh myself. But first, we require space between the scale and the wall in order to access the back panel."

CHAPTER 10

So, Rose knows the trick to removing the panel to retrieve the pennies. I got on my knees, gave the scale a bearhug and pulled. I was surprised when it moved three or four inches. I hadn't expected to move the heavy scale by myself. I remembered Frank's efforts when he brought the scale in from the car.

Rose declared, "That's fine. We don't need much room." She helped me to my feet and asked for the nickel. I found one between two quarters in my change purse and handed it to her. She grinned and gave it back to me. I was a bit puzzled but she moved to the side of the scale and reached behind it.

"Now, Marilee, drop the nickel in the penny slot."

Following directions, I inserted the nickel and listened to the metallic noises from inside the scale. When I heard a click, Rose's hand moved. That metallic snap was unusual. I never heard that peculiar noise when Frank and I used pennies to weigh ourselves. The next thing I saw was Rose standing there holding the back panel.

"Ooh, Rose. How would we have ever known?"

"Someone on the Internet might know about it. But in the earlier models there was a key. After people found a way to duplicate the key, the manufacturer switched to the nickel method. Usually, only the owner knew how to release the panel to get the money. Sometimes there was a fixed second wait."

"How did you know about it, Rose?"

"My second husband owned a five and ten cent store. He told me all the secrets."

"Is the scale full of pennies?" I wondered if there might be some old pennies worth more than a penny, maybe some rare ones.

"We'll have to move the scale farther away from the wall so I can remove the cash box. It's about the size of two cigarette packs and made of cardboard."

"I suppose that's so the money won't make noise when it drops."

Rose nodded, "You're probably right. Do you want to pull the scale farther into the hallway?"

"Sure, I'll use the same technique as before." I grinned, "The brute force-bearhug method." I dropped to my knees, one at a time, moved to the side of the scale and pulled it away from the wall a second time. It seemed easier to move this time, as if it were cooperating to give up money."

I looked in the recess and saw the coin container so I lifted it out and took a look at the contents; a little more than a dozen pennies and two nickels. Someone had accessed the money before but didn't retrieve their nickel, or a five cent piece had been used but the individual didn't know about the trick to open the panel. I dumped the coins on the hall rug so Rose and I could check the dates.

We sat next to each other and examined the little numbers on the pennies. There were about a dozen recent ones from Frank and me and a similar number of older ones from the forties and fifties, but none prior to 1943. The 1943 penny was gray in color. Rose said that copper was limited during the war effort so the pennies were made of steel. Frank probably knew that, but it was news to me. After we had checked out the coins, Rose reached into the scale and said, "Don't be alarmed, Marilee. I'm going to show you something that might startle you."

I was alarmed though. Rose withdrew her right hand holding a small gun.

"Is that real?"

"Yes. It's a twenty-five caliber pistol. It's there in case of a robbery. This scale is just like the one my husband had, it might even be the same one, but if it is, how it got here from Omaha, I have no idea."

"Is it loaded?"

Rose looked more closely at the gun and replied, "Yes, it has three unused bullets."

"Could we try it and see if it shoots?"

"Not a good idea, Marilee. If the barrel is rusty, it might blow up when fired. You better ask your husband to check it out. He knows about guns, doesn't he?"

"Well, I think so, but Ray Meyers would know lots more. He's a hunter. My husband knows how to shoot but that's about all."

"When Frank comes home, show him how to open the access door and extract the gun. Have you got anything in the house needing protection from thieves? If you don't you might consider giving the gun to the police."

"We do have something; my husband has a valuable stamp collection. The gun might come in handy if we have a home invasion." I was thinking of the owners of the yellow sport car. Maybe they are looking for things to steal. No one would know we had a gun; it would be out of sight inside the scale. We'd just need a nickel to get to it. Frank and I will always have to carry nickels, just in case. I bet he's going to be happy that I bought the scale. I'll have to show him what I've learned from Rose today. When I mention that Rose came over, he'll think we played cards. I'll keep it a secret from my bridge buddies . . . loose lips.

"Please put the pistol back in there, Rose, and don't tell anyone that we have a gun in the house, not even my card playing friends. It's our little secret."

"Oh, I won't tell. The fewer people that know, the less chance for accidents." We got up from the floor and moved into the living room. Rose started to put on her coat and I stopped her after she had one arm in it. She was looking outside, probably thinking about the cold walk home.

"Won't you stay and have lunch with me? Afterwards, I'll drive you home. You don't need to be outside walking in the frigid weather. I think the high temperature for today will only be about forty."

She grinned, "That sounds like a very good idea and we can talk about anything, even bridge."

* * *

We made a fresh salad, warmed tea I had made earlier and had cheese slices between crackers for lunch. We must have talked about a hundred different topics. I don't know when I had such a marvelous Saturday. Rose was full of information, undoubtedly due to her many years as a librarian. It was almost two o'clock when I noticed Rose's eyelids were beginning to droop a bit. She hadn't mentioned it but I think her morning walk and our lively discussion for over two hours had drained her physical strength. It was time to take her back home.

We assisted each other with our coats, locked the front door and buckled up in the car. As I started the engine, Rose said, "Let's see if that yellow car is still parked at the curb."

"Tell me where to look for it."

"Two blocks to the left and one block to the right at the corner. It was close to the corner and the stop sign." We travelled in silence as I followed her directions but the corner was devoid of vehicles. No cars or trucks were parked at the curb for the entire block. I continued on, knowing where Evie and Ray lived. I turned into Rose's drive, slowly rolled as close to the house as possible and stopped. Rose was out of the car before I could ask her if I could help her with anything. She came around to my window, which I lowered, and said, "Thank you for a very entertaining day. Maybe we can do it again sometime. Bye now."

I thanked her for showing me how to open the panel on the scale and for the many facets of life discussed during lunch. I watched her as she entered her home, hoping she wouldn't fall. I backed into the street and started home.

I felt exhausted and needed a nap, so I took two straight routes instead of going zigzag through the streets. When I reached the left turn onto my street, I saw the yellow sport car parked on the first side street on the right. I drove around the block in order to make sure it was the same car. I had to see the license plate up close. Sure enough, it said TUF STUF. I wrote down the address in the notepad I kept in the console. I'd come back later and ask the homeowners if they knew the driver of the yellow vehicle.

When I arrived home, I wanted to get on the Internet to check on the old ammunition in the scale gun but Frank's stamp room was locked and he had the only key. I'd have to wait until he came home. After I show him how to open the back panel and the gun, we'll check the barrel for rust and the trustworthiness of the bullets after being inside the scale for what Rose and I estimated to be fifty years or more.

I was greeted by Fred and Blemish when I entered the house. They followed me into the kitchen where I warmed what remained in Mr. Coffee. They stood there waiting for their dinner, but it was still too early, so I gave them a snack and freshened their water. After seeing that yellow car, napping was out of the question, there was no way I could relax, so I sat at the kitchen table sipping reheated coffee and wondered. It suddenly struck me, the owner of that car might be a representative of Mary Kay, selling lipstick, but that car seemed out of place. No, it must be something else, maybe insurance.

If Frank gets back from hunting at a reasonable time, we'll go to that address and ask a few questions. Why would that woman have been peeking into our house? Perhaps the owners of that vehicle were casing the area, trying to find out who had valuables, or maybe I should just forget about it. I decided to shelve the idea and read until Frank came home. I wondered what he will say when I show him that gun.

When six-thirty rolled around and Frank wasn't back yet, I fed the animals and finished off the salad from lunch. For dinner I was going to have lamb chops but I didn't want to cook just for myself. I'll wait for Frank. I hope he's hungry. I turned on the TV and watched a half-hour *Gunsmoke* episode from the 1960s. It was new to me.

Just as the credits were being displayed, car lights played across the vertical blinds. Frank was home. I wonder if Ray got his bear. I'll find out in a few minutes. I turned off the television and went to the kitchen door to meet the celebrated white hunter. I opened the door so Frank wouldn't have to use his key. He would probably leave the telescope in the car until tomorrow; he's undoubtedly tired.

When he saw me, he said, "Hi hon, sorry I'm so late. I hoped to get back before the sun went down, but we had to travel a long distance for Ray to get his bear skin rug."

"So, you guys shot a bear?"

"Yeah. Ray's gonna take it to a taxidermist early tomorrow to help him skin the animal. He'll leave the carcass outside overnight since the temperature will be near freezing. He thinks he can arrange to have the skin made into a rug before he has to be at work."

"Yuk. I bet Evie is glad to have that done somewhere else. What would they do with the meat and bones? I wonder if Safeway could sell the meat?"

Frank laughed, "I don't think so. What did you have for dinner? Any leftovers?"

"I haven't eaten. I was planning on lamb chops. Are you hungry?"

"Sure am. Ray and I ate snacks all afternoon while we waited for Ray's rug to show up." He looked down at his shoes, my eyes followed. "I'm really dirty. I'm gonna leave my shoes outside and clean them off later. Right now, I need a hot shower to wash off the gunk and warm up. Do you mind getting us something to eat by yourself? I'll help as soon as I get cleaned up."

"No, go ahead and hit the shower. I'll start preparing dinner without you. I have some news for you."

"Oh, what's that?"

"It can wait. Get in the shower!"

Twenty minutes later, Frank appeared in his pajamas and shabby bathrobe. I had listened to the shower water and hadn't started cooking the lamb chops until I was sure he was drying off. When he arrived in the kitchen, I served the chops. I made decaffeinated coffee so we wouldn't stay awake all night tossing and turning thinking about the contents of the antique scale.

CHAPTER 11

When we finished eating, Frank assisted with the dirty dishes. I let him load the dishwasher as we talked about our day's activities. He was relieved that Ray had shot his bear for he would no longer have to take part in a displeasing activity.

I asked, "So, your attempts to keep him from getting the bear didn't work?"

"Oh, I chickened out. When we were out there in the wilds, I kinda got into it and all my distracting ideas just evaporated. When he shot the bear, I was kinda proud of chasing around after the animal." He shrugged, "What do you want to tell me?"

"Well, I solved our problem with the scale. I got the back panel off and retrieved the pennies from inside. Wanta see how to remove the panel?"

Frank didn't say anything but slid his chair back and headed for the hallway. I had a vague feeling he wanted to solve the problem himself. Rose and I had pushed the scale back against the wall, so I told Frank, "We need to get the scale away from the wall. Can you move it?"

He nodded and replied, "No problem." He moved it about four inches, put his slippered right foot behind the scale and pushed with his leg moving the scale about a foot into the hallway.

I reacted with a laugh and said, "You did that so easily!"

He smiled and stepped back. "Okay, my dear investigator, show me how to get that panel open."

I grinned, "Got a nickel?"

"In my bathrobe?" He gave me an evil eye.

"That's all right, I've got one." I gave him a nickel from my shirt pocket. "Drop it in the penny slot and listen. When you hear the last metallic sound, press lightly on the back panel."

Frank followed my instructions and in a moment he held the panel in his right hand.

"Okay, now pull out the coin drop-box and give me back my nickel."

He did as I requested and handed me the nickel. "Now reach in the cavity and pull out what your hand contacts." I watched him stick his hand in the hole and search around, withdraw his empty hand and frown, "What? Did I miss getting a prize?"

Of course, I expected him to pull out the small handgun. How could he have missed discovering a pistol? "Step back so I can reach in there." He moved to make room for me to take his place. I felt inside for the gun but it was gone! I suddenly realized Rose took it. I was a bit flustered and said, "Rose took the gun!"

"Gun? What gun?"

"Rose Toliver came over earlier today—this morning. She stayed for lunch and I took her back home around three o'clock. Rose showed me how to open the panel and when we opened it, we discovered a twenty-five caliber handgun inside."

"Rose Toliver; she's the old lady that played bridge with you on Tuesday?"

"Uh-huh, she's the one."

"So, she just appeared at the door before lunch? Did she offer you an apple and you went to sleep? Did you have a bad dream and find a gun?"

"Now you're being ridiculous. Witches are only in fairytales. I don't know what possessed her to take the gun. She even warned me about using old ammunition and to check the barrel for rust. I told her that you don't know much about guns and we would consult with Ray Meyers about the weapon. Rose said there were three bullets in it. She saw that yellow sport car on the way over and we talked about it. Maybe she took the gun for her own protection."

"Okay, I believe you. What do you want to do about it, confront her—and maybe get shot?"

"Frank! She's a nice old lady that wouldn't harm a fly, well…perhaps she would swat flies. I doubt if she ever fired a gun. I think since she saw that yellow sport vehicle, she might have feared for her life. We talked about someone breaking in. I forgot what you told me…you know, not to mention your stamps. I told her you had a valuable collection. She asked if we had any expensive things to protect by having a gun around.

"What about that yellow car?"

"Well, Rose saw it when she walked over here and I saw it again when I was coming back from taking Rose home. I wrote down the address where it was parked. I thought we should go over and ask the people what the driver of that car was doing there. Is it too late tonight?"

Frank laughed and said, "I'm in my pajamas, Marilee. I'm not going anywhere unless our house is on fire."

"Wait right here, I'll get some matches." I pretended to start for the kitchen to get matches from our utility drawer. Frank started laughing and I couldn't help but giggle. I don't know how I came up with that one, Frank is the one who usually cracks funny jokes. My comment was just spontaneous.

Sunday started off as an entirely different day than Saturday, no sign of snow, forty-eight degrees and the weather report suggested the high temperature would be fifty-six by four o'clock. We did our weigh-in to keep up our routine. We had both lost about two pounds in the last week. Frank and I had a lazy morning watching an evangelist on TV instead of going to church and kept warm sitting by the fireplace in our pajamas. I made some hot chocolate at mid-morning and we read the newspapers, the local and the Denver publication. Frank devoured the sports section and I read the society news, what there was of it. I didn't know any of the youngsters getting married. I didn't recognize any of the family names.

We had a lite lunch and set off to do three things, talk to the people in the house where I had seen the yellow sport car and visit Rose to see why she took the gun and recover it. Even though I had never shot a gun before, I wanted one in the house for protection. If in danger, I could point it and pull the trigger; I was sure of that.

Frank drove and I told him where to visit with the homeowners. When we reached the street, he commented, "Oh yeah, ocean is between river and brook. Kind of weird, huh?"

I hadn't noticed the street name before but I agreed with Frank. Someone in the city planner's office had chosen the street names. Maybe they were having a bad day, but what did it matter? We parked at the curb and went to the front door. I knocked to prevent Frank from doing it. I was afraid he would give it a hammer blow with his fist and scare the occupants.

A middle aged woman appeared and said, "Yes? Can I help you?" She was dressed in a house coat, so long I couldn't tell whether she wore slippers, shoes or was in bare feet. We could hear the TV in the background, a football game was on.

"Hello, we are Marilee and Frank Neally and are curious about who was driving that yellow sports car that was parked at your curb yesterday. Are they friends of yours?" The woman was maybe a few years older than us but close to retirement age and only slightly overweight. Her hair was dark brown with streaks of gray.

She smiled, asked us inside and said, "We are the Jacobs, Irene and Del. He's watching a professional football game." She called to him, "Del, come here and meet these people. They want to know who was driving that little yellow car."

Del was dressed in a light-blue sweater and jeans and wore bedroom slippers. He was about six feet tall and thin with fairly long gray hair. He offered his hand to Frank and then to me. Irene then shook hands with us. Irene invited us into the living room and offered us a seat on the sofa. She motioned to Del to mute the TV. He shrugged and followed her directions. They sat at either end of the sofa, Del next to Frank. Irene said, "To answer your question; that was Ms. Corcoran. She said she was a real estate broker and her company wanted to buy our house."

"So, she said she is a realtor. Was she alone? Don't most women realtors come with a partner?"

Del volunteered, "She was alone. She said her partner had come down with Covid but she had to visit people on the weekend when they were at home. She didn't want to bother clients after dinner during the week. I think her name was Shannon." He looked at his wife for confirmation.

She said, "Del would remember her name; I'm not good with names."

I replied, "He remembers names?"

Irene sighed, "Yes, she was a looker." She gave him a dirty look.

Del smiled, "I don't think she was a realtor. She didn't ask about the house . . . you know, square footage, numbers of baths and bedrooms . . .

Irene interrupted, "That's right, she asked if we had insurance on the house and our valuables, if we had a safe for our precious items.

I told her our treasured things were kept in a safety deposit box at the bank." Irene glanced at Del and then us. "That's when she looked at her watch and excused herself. Said she had to go to the pharmacy to pick up drugs for her partner."

"That's about the whole story. I didn't get the name of her company and she didn't leave us any contact information. Don't realtors usually leave their business card?" Del said he was suspicious but didn't know if it was worthwhile to contact someone and who that might be.

Frank nodded and suggested they talk with the police. The cops should know who the woman is and if she is a legitimate real estate agent. We gave the couple the license of the yellow car since they hadn't noticed it and thanked them for talking with us. We excused ourselves and returned to our now cold car.

As we got in, I said, "It's cold in here!" Frank quickly started the engine and turned on the heater, full blast. He then touched something on the dash and I felt the seat warming my rear and thighs. Frank got on his knees on the driver's seat, reached into the back seat and handed me a small wool blanket. I remember sitting on it when we went to a Colorado football game a year ago. I spread the blanket over my lap and legs.

Frank grinned and quizzed, "Comfy?"

I answered back, "Could you start a fire?" and we both laughed.

As we pulled away from the curb, Frank queried, "Okay, where does Rose live?"

"Right across the street from Evie and Ray."

"Great! We're more than halfway there already. Does she have a driveway?"

"Yes, dear, it's a regular house, kind of like a cottage, a little bit larger. I don't think she drives. She walked over to our place yesterday morning."

"It's probably good that she doesn't drive—she's in her nighties?"

"Very funny. Yes, she's in her nineties. I believe she's ninety-three."

"Pretty spry to walk from here to our house in the cold." Frank pulled into Rose's driveway and stopped. We got out of the car and walked to the front door. I hesitated for a moment, knocked and we waited for several seconds before hearing footsteps.

The door opened slowly. Rose was using the door as a shield and peered at Frank and then saw me. "Oh! It's you, Marilee, and this must be Frank. Please come in."

Frank opened the screen door and we entered the foyer. I shut the door behind us. Rose said, "Follow me. Take off your coats and stay awhile. Put your coats anywhere you like. I think I know why you are here." She waved us to her sofa and we sat down. She sat in a large, padded rocker. She must have been reading, there was a marker in a thick book sitting on a TV tray next to her. A big floor lamp with a light-blue shade towered over her right shoulder.

I broke the silence, "I wanted to ask you why you took the gun. Frank thought I was hallucinating about the gun when he reached into the compartment and found nothing."

"Well, I just borrowed the gun. I suppose I should have asked you but after we talked, I figured it would be better for me to take the gun to a friend and have him clean it for you. I'll bring it back on Tuesday when we meet for bridge. I hope that is okay."

"So, you don't have it now?"

"That's right. I took it to Jonathan Fredericks after you brought me home. I called Citywide Rides and had the driver take me to Jonathan. He looked it over and told me it wouldn't take much to clean and guarantee it was in working order. He didn't even charge me. He used to come to the library and study when he was a high schooler. I've known him and his wife for nearly thirty years. They have two teenagers, a girl and a boy."

CHAPTER 12

Frank stood and reached for his coat but Rose motioned for him to stay seated. "Please, won't you stay for a while? Can I offer you something to drink? I have some tasty peanut butter cookies."

"Coffee would be nice, but we're on a diet and have given up treats. We'll pass on the cookies, thank you anyway."

Rose replied, "Oh, that's right. That's why you bought that old scale. Well, I'll get you some coffee. Do you take it straight? I have some of that imitation creamer. I don't think it has many calories."

I motioned to Frank to sit down. "Do you want me to assist?"

"That would be nice."

I followed Rose into the kitchen. As she got cups and saucers from her cupboard, she asked, "Is Frank an impatient man?"

"Not usually unless I interrupt his important activities. He bought a telescope recently and is determined to learn all about astronomy. He's waiting for a cloudless night when it's not too cold."

"I wish him good luck—I mean with the cold. I believe we are in for a very cold winter. It won't start warming up until next April. I visited Mt. Palomar once. I'm also interested in astronomy. The book I'm reading is a compendium of papers about dark matter and dark energy—very confusing to even very bright people."

She had me perplexed and my face must have shown my confusion. I had never heard of the things she had just referred to. Frank had mentioned black holes to me the other day and I was having trouble with that concept. I hope Rose doesn't bring those ideas to our bridge club meetings. I'll ask Frank if he knows about dark matter and dark energy. He'll probably ask me if I'm hallucinating again.

While my brain was fogging over, Rose poured the coffee and I carried Frank's and my drinks into the other room. Frank was leaning back on the sofa with his eyes closed but abruptly sat up straight when Rose and I joined him with the dark roast brew.

"Did I hear you ladies mention astronomy?"

I handed Frank a cup of coffee and replied, "I was telling Rose about your telescope and she mentioned she was reading about dark something—I didn't understand."

He took a sip of coffee and said, "I don't understand those things either. I'm trying to figure out black holes and different types of galaxies. I need a much bigger telescope in order to gather more light. That stuff is mind distorting. I regret not taking physics in high school. I stopped taking science classes after biology. I'm good at math but without physics I struggle with the physical sciences."

We talked about the planets and Rose asked Frank to tell her when he was observing Jupiter and Saturn. She would like to take a look. He promised to invite her over but it would be cold and she would have to dress warmly. That's when he said he wanted to get a bigger telescope, one with a large mirror. I could see Rose was getting excited about the idea. She had seen Saturn with an eight inch reflector once and found it transfixing. It looked like the planet was not moving and hanging in space. As I listened to them talking, I was beginning to get more interested in Frank's latest pursuit. I sat there thinking how I could get involved; maybe I could get a camera and take pictures of heavenly bodies.

But then I began to wonder. Was Frank going to share his interest with me? I hope so. When I mentioned earlier in the day that we were going to visit Rose to ask about the gun, he was reserved, a bit skeptical about the whole idea. But now as I see him engrossed in discussion with Rose, his enthusiasm for astronomy is evident. I want to join in. I'll see how he feels when we get home, maybe on the way back. I wonder if there is a local group of amateur astronomers, an organization where I could learn about taking pictures through a telescope. Frank should know if there is such a group. I think he once mentioned getting a camera.

I heard Frank call to me, "Marilee, are you ready to go? I think Rose wants to take a nap and get with her regular Sunday routine." I glanced where they were talking and Rose reacted, "I'm glad you came over today. It was so enjoyable. Please tell me when you are out observing the planets, especially if you get a bigger telescope. And Marilee, I'll bring your gun back on Tuesday when we have our next card playing time."

"Please don't tell anyone you are bringing me a gun. I don't want anyone else to know about it or how to get at it. We'll keep it a secret, only four people will know. Okay?"

Rose nodded, "I understand. I think that's a good idea." She moved over to our coats and helped me with mine as Frank donned his new heavy jacket and slowly made his way to the door. I followed, walking backwards and said goodbye to Rose. "I'll see you day after tomorrow. If you can't get a ride with Evelyn, call me and I'll come and pick you up. Oh, let me give you my phone number."

Rose rushed over to her desk, grabbed a pen and waited for me to recite my number. As she wrote it on a scrap of paper I asked for her number. I entered it in my purse notebook and said, "Goodbye Rose, see you on Tuesday."

When I reached the car and scooted onto the passenger cushion, Frank turned on the seat warmer and tucked the blanket over my legs. He started the engine and we backed onto the street, honked twice, and started home.

"So, Frank, what do you think of Rose?"

"She's very intelligent and certainly isn't suffering from Alzheimer's."

"That never occurred to me. I think you enjoyed talking about astronomy."

"Sure did. I learned a lot from her. Imagine, we came over to find a gun and I found out important details about my new hobby."

"For example . . ."

"She told me I should get an equatorial mount, not a Dobsonian."

"What's the difference?" I had never heard of either one.

Frank was so devoted to the explanation, he drove past our driveway.

"Frank, that was our drive."

"Oh! So, it was." He laughed and drove around the block. I looked at him and chuckled, "I guess we'd better leave the technical stuff until we're in the house and relaxed. Besides, I have an important question for you. I hope you like the idea."

He glanced at me as he stopped the car, "When have I ever not liked an idea of yours?" He grinned and blurted out, "Don't answer that."

The animals greeted us when we entered the house. We had been away for almost five hours, which was unusual for us on a Sunday. Fred and Blemish undoubtedly noticed our absence. Frank restarted the logs in the fireplace as I hung up our coats. I went in the kitchen thinking of hot chocolate but started Mr. Coffee instead. Our pets were following me around, so I decided to give them their dinner a little earlier than normal.

Frank joined me and asked, "What were you going to ask me?"

"You know how much I like taking pictures when we're on trips. If you get a bigger telescope, how would it be if I get a camera to take astronomical pictures? Would you think I was butting into your new hobby"?

He thought for at least ten seconds before answering. "You know, that is a good idea. We can be together and freeze our behinds in the cold dark outdoors this winter. Let's go online and search for some good deals. I bought a copy of the latest *Astronomy* magazine today; we can check the ads too."

I was beginning to worry about the costs of the new equipment but Frank didn't show any signs of hesitancy. I think he had already investigated the expense of a larger telescope. What I didn't know was whether he had considered getting a camera for astrophotography. I added that word to my vocabulary on Saturday. Rose is packed full of information.

While we ate dinner, we talked about telescopes, bridge and insurance agents. Frank said he would call Sheriff Abbott from the post office and ask about the insurance woman. During our visit with Rose, I pondered whether Miss Shannon was truly a real estate agent. Her actions just didn't quite sit right, so I was pleased that Frank was continuing the investigation.

Monday seemed to flash by and at about three o'clock in the afternoon, I was startled by the phone ringing. I recognized the voice immediately; it was Sheri Sandborne.

"Hi Sher, are you getting ready for tomorrow's game?"

"That's why I called. I can't come. Can you get a sub?"

"Sorry you won't be here. Did something just come up?"

"I scheduled a mammogram and forgot about it. The hospital lab called about ten minutes ago to remind me. I'm glad you are at home."

"Do you suspect a problem?"

"No, just a regular checkup."

"Oh, that's good. Well, don't worry, Rose will be coming with Evie, so we'll still have a foursome. Thanks for the call. We'll see you next Tuesday at Dotty's. The week after, we'll be at your place."

I could hear her chuckling. *"That will give me two weeks to clean the house."*

I replied, "I have less than twenty-four hours. I have to vacuum and do some dusting tonight. I'll have Frank get out the card tables. Have fun at the lab tomorrow."

Sheri forced out a laugh, *"Thanks, Marilee. It's always cold in the lab, and I'll be half naked."*

"Sounds like my experience. Maybe they'll have changed and have the heat turned up. Let me know the results, okay?"

"Okay, bye now. See you a week from tomorrow."

"Bye Sher."

I called Evie, explained Sheri's situation and made sure Rose would get a ride. After the call, I read for about fifteen minutes and started preparations for dinner. I hoped to get some information about that realtor chic from Frank. I hope he remembered to talk to the sheriff. That yellow car and sexy young woman seemed etched into my brain. I shook off the images and went in the kitchen after turning on the television for some background noise.

It was getting dark out when Frank pulled into the driveway. I glanced at the clock, 5:45. Salad and coffee were ready, all that remained was to warm the vegetables and cook the salmon. We would be ready to eat by the time Frank changed from his work clothes. I laid out a pair of jeans and a Colorado sweatshirt earlier. I had put his bathrobe in the washing machine but forgot to turn it on. I rushed into the utility room and started the machine as Frank came into the house with a handful of mail.

"How's my favorite wife?"

"Just peachy, dear. Would you please get the card tables out of the closet. Tomorrow's bridge day. I put some clothes for you on the bed. Your robe is in the wash. Dinner's almost ready."

I hadn't given Frank a chance to say anything but we'd have a good discussion while we ate. He must have listened attentively because the next sounds came from the closet door and then the bathroom. I assumed he got the card tables out and then decided to shower.

Gauging how long Frank was going to be in the shower was not one of my refined skills, there were just too many variables. I assumed about ten minutes, so I started the salmon. Luck was with me. As the filets were finishing, Frank appeared in a sweatshirt and jeans but barefoot.

"Where do you want the tables?"

"Just lean them against the sofa. Don't bother to extend the fold-up legs. Thank you . . . dinner's ready."

We ate quietly, only uttering a few words for several minutes before Frank said, "I called the sheriff this morning at ten o'clock and he pawned me off on deputy Durham. He's a new guy that joined the force about two weeks ago; first name is Ronald. He said he would check on the realtor named Shannon for me. He called back at one-thirty and told me there was a Shannon working for Wild West Realty. They haven't had any complaints about her."

"Wild West Realty? They must be out of Denver; I've never heard of them."

"I think he said Wild West was listed as a company in Boise."

"That's why I've never heard of them. Seems kind of strange they would be in Colorado, doesn't it?"

Frank stopped chewing and looked at me. "Yeah, that is kinda strange. Summit's Way is off the beaten path. Maybe they're trying something new, like stealing from homeowners and getting a cut of the insurance funds." Grinning, he took another bite of salmon.

CHAPTER 13

Frank extracted his wallet from his left rear pocket and pulled out a yellow Post-It note with scribbling on it. The innocent piece of paper triggered an image of that empty yellow car parked at the curb. It was just a flash through my mind and Frank's next contribution got my rapt attention.

"Oh, guess what happened today."

"You found a wooden nickel?"

"No, this is serious stuff. Ray Meyers called me."

"About his rug?"

"Listen, dear. Forget about that damned rug. He called me about getting a telescope for the city."

"I don't understand. What do you mean for the city?"

"Well, I asked him if there was a star gazing group in town and he said there is. It's managed by Professor Mark Tyler, a retired physicist from the Air Force Academy. He welcomes new members and wants to construct an observatory and install a sixteen inch telescope. He's even talked to the city council and they like the idea. They think it would be great to have for students and community star nights."

I looked at Frank a little in disbelief. How could this have happened without our knowledge? Nothing was in the newspaper. "So, what's the catch?"

"An estimated cost for the entire undertaking would be over thirty grand. Each member of the group would need to donate a minimum of a thousand dollars. The city has promised five thousand and would pay for power and sewage, that's probably another five thousand."

"Sewage?"

"Yep. The structure would have to contain restrooms."

"And where would this location be? In town?"

"Not in town. Too much light interference, you know, streetlights and business signs. The city is going to ask for the donation of a small parcel of land outside the city limits."

"How did Ray get all this information?"

Frank swallowed and cleared his throat, "The retired university teacher came into the bank and asked Ray about setting up an account for the observatory. The professor wanted to call the observatory complex Summit's Way to the Stars. At first Ray was a bit skeptical, but after talking with Doctor Tyler for about ten minutes, Ray offered him his utmost cooperation. I could tell by Ray's voice over the phone, he was extremely enthusiastic. Ray called me a few minutes after the professor left the bank. Ray wants us to join in the venture."

Frank looked at me as if to ask if I was willing to go along with him and donate a thousand dollars. I had to ask a couple of questions.

"Then you're not going to get a new telescope? How much would it cost us if you bought a new one and we bought a camera?"

He grinned, "A lot more than a thousand, maybe three or four grand. I think it's a good deal for us, although we would have to share time with others for using the scope."

"When would it be ready, a year from now?"

"Yeah, at least a year, maybe two years, but that's about the time I retire and I would have something to shift into with my time and energy."

"Well, what about your stamp collection?"

He laughed, "That's where the thousand will come from. I don't want to spend from our savings. That money is for more important things. I have one set of stamps that will get us a thousand dollars. We'll go into Denver and sell it to a dealer."

"Did Ray tell you when he wanted the money?"

"Nope, he just encouraged me to deposit the money in the observatory's account to indicate we want to take part in the construction."

"Are Ray and Evelyn going to do it, too?"

"Uh-huh, and the bank is going to donate another five thousand. Altogether, the account will have about twenty-seven thousand dollars, plenty enough to start construction. Dr. Tyler will contact the property owners of three possible sites. The donor, of course, will get a tax write-off."

"This sounds like a good deal for the community and each of the donating members. I kinda wish the bridge club could do something similar but we are just four sixty-plus wives and a ninety-year-old retired librarian."

"Don't think of it that way, dear. You gals can be involved by supplying food and sharing information with the schools. I'm guessing all of the members want to get the young people involved. They might sell hot chocolate and cupcakes at star night open house when everyone can look at the moon and one or two of the planets. We can photograph galaxies, too."

"Oh, do you remember? Rose wants to see Saturn through a big telescope."

Frank nodded, "When we get the observatory running, she'll be our first honored guest."

After dinner, Frank set up the card tables and I vacuumed the living room and hallway rugs. I tossed him a dust cloth and we wiped off every item we could get our hands on. Afterwards, I gave the room a giant spray with Lilac Scent air freshener. Frank remarked, "When you use that stuff, make sure my stamp room door is shut. Those air-borne molecules will probably damage my stamps."

I hadn't considered the spray might damage his collection, but he was probably right. Frank took a whiff of the living room air and waved his hands. The odor wasn't to his liking. I put the spray can under the kitchen sink and followed Frank to the bedroom. Fifteen minutes later, we were in bed and I turned out the lights.

We had an interesting Tuesday morning. While Frank was still in his pajamas, he went in the stamp room and turned on the computer. While he was fooling around, I got dressed and started breakfast after a brief visit to the scale. Another pound lost forever, I hoped.

Frank yelled from his stamp room, "Do you have anything planned for Saturday?"

"No!" I yelled back and began to wonder what he was planning. Something to do with the observatory, I'll bet. All I could think of was that he wasn't planning on another bear hunt. I dropped a couple slices of bread in the toaster and set the table. I should have asked Frank if he wanted some oatmeal, but I started it anyway. I was humming a Christmas carol as I watched kids walking by and didn't hear Frank sit down at the table. When I turned around, he was buttering toast.

I asked, "Why did you want to know if I had plans for Saturday?'

"I was checking on the dealer offers for those stamps I want to sell. I can get a little over a thousand from Bob's Bargain Stamps in Denver. Want to go with me? It would take all afternoon—two hours up, an hour with the dealer, and two hours back. If you want to do some shopping, we could stay over, or come back later in the evening. What do you think?"

"As long as you do the city driving, I'm all for it. We can get some of our winter gear, especially snowshoes. But let's get an early start and hope the weather cooperates. We can have a nice lunch at Le Restaurant Alpin and then sell those stamps."

"You mean we're skipping McDonalds? All I want is a cheeseburger and coffee—no fries."

I snickered, "All I want is a European salad, anything else will add to my weight."

Frank became serious, "Make up a list of items for us to purchase in the city, meaningful things; like something we've always wanted for Christmas. Maybe a special decoration that will remind us of getting the funds to assist in the creation of an observatory. We'll talk about it tonight, okay?" He pushed back from the table, slipped into his suit coat and headed for the car. As the door closed, I heard him say, "Later, Marilee."

I said, "Bye," but he probably didn't hear me. I sat there at the table for a few minutes thinking about what he said, but we already had a nativity scene and so many strings of old lights we would trip a circuit breaker if we had them all plugged in at the same time. I've got three and a half days to come up with something clever, maybe I'll notice something in one of our magazines. Frank might have an idea or two by tonight, maybe a special star ornament for a treetop.

At a quarter to one I was ready for the girls to start arriving, so I decided to kill some time thumbing through our latest monthlies, glancing at the pictures looking for an appropriate decoration. Unfortunately,

Christmas was still too far off and I didn't see anything that generated any ideas. The November issues would be a better source, but they hadn't begun to arrive yet. Maybe something will pop up before Saturday.

Dotty arrived first carrying a Tupperware container of brownies. When I stared at what she was carrying, she volunteered, "They're brownies, but I used unsweetened chocolate and artificial sweetener. The calories are extremely low. I'll bet you can have at least one, Mari."

I grinned, "When I deal, I'll do some extra shuffling and burn off the calories. I've got Mr. Coffee working in the kitchen."

She snickered, "Does Frank know you have a man in the kitchen making coffee?"

We both laughed. "Good one, Dot, don't tell anyone."

There was car noise in the driveway and I watched Evie and Rose coming toward our front door.

"Dotty, would you please get the door. Evie and Rose are here."

I was preparing a tray for coffee and the brownies. It was all I could do to keep from gobbling one of those delicious looking snacks, but I was sure Dotty would notice one was missing. I altered the image in my head to that of a European salad I was expecting on Saturday.

I did my best to imitate a server and waltzed into the living room with my largest serving tray.

I set it on the second card table and instructed everyone to sit. Before we started play, I wanted to tell them about the planned observatory. Ray probably told Evie about it, but the others might not have heard.

Dotty wasn't too interested, but Rose was delighted. When I saw her eyes light up, I noticed she was holding a shoebox in her lap. I assumed it held the gun. Surely, she wouldn't show the girls that gun, contrary to what I wanted.

I asked her, "Rose, what do you have in that box? Is it more treats?"

"Oh my, no. It's a jigsaw puzzle." She removed the lid and showed us the puzzle pieces, then explained, "I've had this in my bedroom closet for years. I don't know where it came from but there was a note inside stating all the pieces were present. I've wondered what the picture is. I thought you ladies might help me assemble it."

Dotty was looking closely at the jumbled pieces and remarked, "There must be a thousand pieces, Rose. It will take several meetings to put it all together and we don't have a picture to follow."

Rose looked disappointed. "Then you don't want to do it? Well, that's okay, it was just an idea, something different than playing bridge all the time."

"No, I didn't mean that. I was just speaking out loud about the difficulty. I haven't assembled a puzzle in years."

Evie and I glanced at each other and smiled. I think we had the same thought. She nodded and I said, "I think it's a good idea. We can play bridge any time but this is a change of pace. I'm curious about the puzzle picture. I wonder what it is all about, a street scene, mountains, a boat? If there are any people, how are they dressed? It might tell us how old the puzzle is. Perhaps we'll find a manufacturer's trademark."

Evie made another suggestion, "Let's play bridge for a while and then start work on the mystery. I'm curious to find out if cars are in the picture. They might give us a clue to the age of the puzzle."

Rose reacted with a big smile, "That sounds great. Let's play bridge."

Card playing busied us for about an hour. We had all dealt at least once when Rose stood and announced, "I'm about to explode, too much coffee for my weak bladder. May I use your bathroom, Marilee?"

"Go ahead, Rose, we'll take a break now. Brownies and coffee should hit the spot. I'll use the porcelain palace after you."

Dotty chimed in, "I'm next!"

Evie said, "I'm afraid to laugh, I might have an accident. Don't any of you say anything funny!"

I glanced at Dotty. She raised her right eyebrow and grinned. I think she wanted Evie to wet her pants.

I decided to risk eating one of the brownies so I started to nibble on the smallest one on the tray. I listened for Rose to exit the bathroom. When I heard the door, I jumped to my feet, hurried down the hallway and whispered to Rose.

"Did you return the gun?"

She whispered back, "I'm not strong enough to move the scale, so I put it in your linen closet—under the stack of bath towels. Three bullets are still in it. Jonathan said they should work, they're original manufactured ammunition."

"Thanks, Rose. I hope I never have to use it. I'll put it in the scale when Frank comes home."

She nodded and went back to the living room.

When we had all used the facilities, I shifted the refreshment tray to the kitchen and commented, "I'm moving the brownies into the kitchen. They are too tempting." I was surprised when the girls all agreed with me. I think they didn't want to sabotage my new diet. But then I speculated, were they all of the opinion I was overweight?

CHAPTER 14

As I returned to the living room, I saw Rose invert the puzzle box, dumping all those irregular pieces on our playing table. She casually tossed the empty container onto the sofa and sat in one of the chairs, her eyes glued to the pile of puzzle pieces.

She looked up at us, "Let's turn over the upside-down pieces so they are face up, then we'll pick out the straight edged ones and see what we can do with them on the other table."

We were enslaved for about twenty minutes finding all the border pieces and a similar period assembling them to make a rectangle about half the size of the card table surface. Dotty never sat down. She seemed to have a knack for seeing where and how the edges fit together. The rest of us let her take over and put the framing pieces in the correct positions. Rose remarked that Dotty's ability came from fantastic eyesight, color recognition, and nimble fingers. The rest of us agreed, Dotty was the best card shuffler of us all.

As Dotty worked on the border edges, she commented, "I think I just see things from a different vantage point." I stood up and tried to help, but I couldn't match what Dotty was doing. I thought I saw where a strip of five pieces went and began to move them but Dotty slapped my hands away saying, "No, Marilee, those pieces have to be blue."

I pulled my hands back and said, "Sorry, I thought the shape was right. I forgot to check the color."

Evie suggested, "Let's take a picture of the completed part and see if we can find something on the Internet that matches. Wouldn't it be nice to have a picture to follow?"

Rose and I agreed. The three of us took pictures to take home to search the Net using our computers. We couldn't get on the Net with phones, no reception as usual. Dotty continued building the edges of the puzzle.

Evie said, "Look at the time gals, we'd better stop for now and continue next week."

Dotty stepped back, straightening and flexing her shoulders and back. She looked at me. "What are we going to do with what we have achieved? Are we going to start all over next time?"

That was a pertinent question. Although I didn't know if it would work, I proposed an idea. I remembered Frank having some large sheets of cardboard used to keep full sheets of stamps from being bent over. The cardboard could be taped together and slid under the puzzle pieces, keeping them intact. I told the girls my plan and they thought it would work. I would then transport the partial puzzle to the next meeting.

Evie asked, "What about all the pieces we just turned over? Will we have to do that all over?"

I reacted, "I'll have Frank fix two large sheets of cardboard. I think he'll enjoy the challenge."

We all laughed when I said that because I rolled my eyes.

Dotty was next to sponsor our group so she said, "I'll have some brownies for you when we assemble for bridge and puzzle assembling. Shall we devote the same time to each activity, an hour for each?"

Evie grinned, "You'd better bake a new batch of brownies, Dot. The ones you brought will be like rocks in a week."

Dotty replied, "Don't worry, I'll make a new batch. I'll save the ones from today for trick or treaters."

I answered, chuckling, "You'll have lawsuits and dental bills to pay, dear."

We all knew she was joking but I had to comment with more banter. The girls took their time leaving, expressing their delight in the afternoon. Dotty joined me for a last remark, "Please bring the puzzle over in plenty of time for us to get everything set up. I don't have three card tables. We'll use the dining room table for the puzzle."

"Okay, I'll come at least a half hour early. You can help me get the materials out of my car. I think it will be a two woman job so nothing gets scrambled."

Rose and Evie had gone to their car and were sitting with the motor running, I assumed they were waiting for the heater to become fully functional. Dotty and I stepped out on the front porch and waved to the others as they drove off. I didn't have my coat so I was starting to shiver.

"I'll see you next Tuesday, Dot. Have a save ride home." I turned around quickly and hustled into the warmth of the foyer. I watched from behind the storm door as Dotty waved and beeped her horn when she pulled away from the curb. I waved back but it was too late for her to see the motion of my arm. I was saddened to see them go after having more than two hours of fun playing cards and fitting puzzle pieces together. I would have to see if Frank can help me figure out a way to transport the partly assembled jigsaw mystery. I hope he's wearing his clever hat tonight.

As I passed by the puzzle on the way to the kitchen, I stopped to ponder what Dotty had done. From the assembled edges, I imagined the picture was a coastal scene. It looked as if sky and water were going to be major components. I took a quick glance at the pieces on the other table and could see a number of white and brown colors. I continued on to the kitchen and started getting ready to prepare dinner—lasagna.

Fortunately, I didn't have to make the main course from scratch. I had purchased a family size frozen dinner the day Dotty and I bumped into each other at the grocery store. Instead of making a fresh salad, I decided to heat some frozen asparagus. The microwave was going to get a workout tonight. I made some fresh coffee and sat down with my bridge book. I couldn't concentrate, so I flipped on the TV and listened to the four-thirty news. The weather lady said Denver was expected to get a couple inches of snow tomorrow—just what Frank and I needed. I wonder if he'll still want to make the trip. I expected him to be home in thirty minutes.

My phone rang. It was Frank saying he would be a half-hour late. He took the car in for servicing to make sure it was in good shape for the journey to Denver. He was about to leave the post office to go to the service center to pick up our vehicle. He asked if he should pick up anything for dinner. I said no, we were in good shape for tonight.

"But I have a project for you. I'll show you when you get home. I also want to talk about the object from the scale." I didn't want to say gun over the phone. These days, who knows who might be listening? After watching the news, I imagined the FBI might show up, break down our door and accuse us of selling illegal drugs and guns.

Frank pulled into our driveway as I was taking the boxed dinner from the refrigerator freezing compartment. I was reading the instructions for microwave cooking when he came into the house.

"What's for dinner, Mari?"

"Do you like asparagus? I don't remember."

"It's alright with salt and butter, but what's the main course?"

"Lasagna, with beef and cheese. It's one of those frozen dinners. The picture on the container looks good." I gave him a big smile.

He returned a frown, "We'll see. Something new is not always good, but I'm willing to try it. The portrayal on the box is always better than the contents. Now, what was it about the gun?"

"Rose returned it. She put it under the towels in the linen closet. I've been thinking about where to put it if we ever need it in an emergency—the scale is not a good place. Rose knows about it."

"You think Rose will blab it around?"

"I don't think so but she just might inadvertently let it slip out. And that guy that checked out the gun, Johnathan. He might know about it. I don't know what Rose told him."

Frank nodded, "You're probably right. Let me think about it while we eat. Call me when dinner is ready, I'll be in my stamp room. Some new issues arrived today."

I rechecked the lasagna box for microwave directions and it indicated eight to ten minutes on high. I put the asparagus in some water on the stove so the main dish and the vegetable would be ready simultaneously. After eight minutes, I shouted down the hall to Frank, "It's ready, wash your hands."

When Frank arrived at the table, the microwave beeped four times. The lasagna was ready. We had an enjoyable dinner; the pasta was really good. Frank and I agreed that we should get some more but he had me promise to skip the asparagus, he'd rather have cauliflower or broccoli. I didn't think the asparagus was bad but Frank was not a fan.

When we finished eating and were drinking coffee, he commented, "I moved the gun into the stamp room. I want you to find it."

"So, you want me to play hide and seek."

"Well, I want to find out if the gun is in a good place and not obvious."

Frank must have thought of an ideal location for the gun before we started eating dinner. He undoubtedly figured out a place when he was mounting the new issues in his albums. He was adamant about visitors having clean hands when in his sanctified room for stamps. I rinsed my hands at the kitchen sink, dried them thoroughly and headed down the hall with Frank a few feet behind.

"Are your hands clean and completely dry?"

I wanted to slug him but I patiently turned around, grabbed his hands so he could check them. I passed the test. I started looking in the obvious places, the desk drawers. I found nothing but stamp collector's supplies. I didn't realize so much junk was in those compartments. I stood up and scanned the walls, nothing but shelves of stamp albums, a digital clock and a barometer. Ye gods! A barometer? Was he actually checking the barometric pressure? I hadn't paid much attention to the walls the few times I had ventured into his hobby room. I must have noticed the barometer before but had never *really* seen it.

"Does that barometer work?"

"Sure does. I use it to warn of oncoming storms and humidity changes. I then check the weather reports." He chuckled, "It's more of a wall decoration than anything. I like the wood and gold color around the dial."

"Oh, well, it's too small to hide a gun in it." I completed another survey of the walls and stood there thinking. In movies, where had I seen guns hidden? I moved his chair back from the desk, dropped to my knees and looked below the middle drawer. Nope, nothing was taped to the bottom. While I was down, I checked the bottom of the chair. Nothing. I rose to my feet, looked at Frank and asked, "Okay, you've got me. Where's the gun?"

He pointed to the shelf within reach at the side of the desk. "Look in the slipcase for the Great Britain album."

I moved to the thick wooden rack and slid the designated album case off the shelf. There was no album inside but there was a gun.

"Where did you put the Great Britain album?"

"Never had one. I bought that slip case at a garage sale for fifty cents. I was going to use it as a spare if one of my U.S. cases got damaged. It would be a temp until I was able to pick up a new proper one in Denver."

"So, there is a reason for your madness. Very clever of you, Frank. I would never have thought to look in that case. I thought the cases would all be occupied by stamp albums."

"That's what I had decided but you did perform a good search."

I smiled, "Thanks. Now I wonder what else you have hidden from me."

He snickered, "I guess you'll never know."

After I replaced the gun in the slip case, Frank put his arm around my waist and escorted me back to the living room for a celebratory night cap.

CHAPTER 15

Nightcaps were now rare, especially since starting our new diet, but Frank got out a couple of small juice glasses and added about three ounces of wine to each. Maybe a little bit of fermented juice will help me sleep tonight. I have to admit putting the gun in that album box was a good, even a great idea. Who would ever think of searching for a gun in what appeared to contain a stamp album? Then I remembered seeing a movie with a gun hidden in a book with the pages cut out. Maybe the new generation of thieves hasn't seen that movie.

Frank had finally noticed the puzzle. He looked at what we had accomplished and asked, "What's with the puzzle? Have you ladies gotten tired of playing bridge?"

"Not really, Rose brought it today. She mentioned having it in her closet for years but didn't know what the picture was. We decided to put it together in addition to playing cards. But now we have a problem that the girls want you to solve."

He thought for a couple of seconds. "You want me to figure out the picture?"

I shook my head, "Nope. We want you to figure out a way to transport the puzzle from one location to another without fouling up our progress."

He grinned, "Glue it to the table and take the table from place to place."

I replied, "Okay, no more wine for you. Now, please come up with a serious solution. Okay?"

He chuckled, "Get me that cookie sheet, the one that's completely flat."

It suddenly occurred to me what he was thinking. I took the wine glasses to the sink and pulled open the drawer below the oven. I had to move several pie tins and a large pizza serving tray to access and extract the metal cookie sheet. The process was a bit noisy but rewarding. I left the drawer open and took the metal sheet to Frank.

As I took the item into the living room, I almost started to yell at him. He was taking the top and bottom of the puzzle apart, right in the middle. I kept quiet, almost ready to bite my tongue, assuming he would explain his procedure and not completely ruin what the group had assembled. Before I could say anything, I watched him slowly slide the cookie sheet under the puzzle pieces from the side.

When half the puzzle pieces were on the flat metal sheet, he went to his stamp room and returned with six thin sheets of 8½ by 11 cardboard. His next words were, "I need some Scotch tape."

Was he going to stick the pieces to the cardboard? Previously he had kidded me with the glue idea, now what? I fished the little dispenser from the kitchen utility drawer and tossed it to him.

"Thank-you."

I watched him tape two of the cardboard sheets together and place them on the dining room table. Then he took the cookie sheet and slid half the puzzle edges onto the cardboard. A few pieces came apart but were immediately rejoined. He used the same procedure with the other half puzzle edges and placed the second arrangement on top of the first.

He glanced at me, smiled and put the last two taped together cardboards on top of the others.

"There you have it, a double-decker puzzle sandwich—ready for travel after the edges are taped."

I gave Frank a round of applause and said, "What about the other pieces?"

He scratched his chin and replied, "Dump them in the box and dump them out again. Only half will be inverted and will need to be turned over."

I gave him a questioning look.

He shook his head and said, "Probability."

I understood and followed with, "Oh, I get it. Thank-you for the great idea."

Then he said, "Happy wife, happy life." I could have slugged him.

I slept soundly. I guess the slight wind helped, or was it that the method to transport the puzzle was solved? I'd have to remember to take the tape with me, just in case. I weighed in when I got up and noticed no change in weight in the last twenty-four hours. It couldn't have been the wine, but the culprit had to have been the lasagna. I'll watch what I eat today but not starve. I'll call Dotty and tell her transporting the puzzle problem has been solved. I figured Frank would come up with a solution. I realized I would have to transport the cardboard sandwich in the back of the SUV so it would lay flat.

Wednesday, Frank came into the kitchen for breakfast dressed for work and exhibiting a scowl. "The damned weather is going to be nasty on Saturday. I'm thinking we might stay home."

"That's courtesy of the computer? An inch or two of snow shouldn't be a problem. It's too early for a blizzard, isn't it?"

He nodded, reached into his pocket and withdrew a key. "Here's the key to the stamp room but please keep it locked. I'd rather not have any of your lady friends wandering in there looking for the bathroom."

"Don't worry. They all know where the bathroom is located." I held the key in both hands so he could see it and said, "I'll keep this on a necklace so it doesn't get misplaced."

He smiled, "Okay, even when you shower. It shouldn't rust."

I wasn't too sure he was joking but I said, "I'll sew a small pocket into my bra so I won't develop an allergy to the metal."

He frowned, "You're kidding, right?"

"No, I'm serious."

He leaned against the counter, finished his coffee, uttered, "See you later, dear," and was out the door.

I called after him, "Your overcoat!"

He turned and whispered, "It's in the car." He waved, "Bye."

After rinsing the few morning dishes, I called Dotty and told her about Frank's idea for moving the puzzle from place to place. As we gabbed, I wondered if Dotty had a cookie sheet like the one Frank used. I asked her. I didn't want to haul my cookie sheet unless absolutely necessary.

"Not a problem, Marilee, you don't need to bring yours. I want to tell you something. I had Dale buy a new card table. One of our two old ones is beyond it's useful years. We'll Have a nice flat surface for the puzzle. See you on Tuesday. Bye."

After hanging up, I checked the latest catalogs from the big stores in Denver. I think I must have spent an inordinate amount of time looking through a thick one from *Lofty Denver Boutique*. I was afraid my magic marker was going to dry up before I finished searching the pages. The name of the store is a misnomer, the specialty shop is actually an enormous building housing at least ten small businesses. I closed the last page, looked at my watch and realized it was time for lunch.

Coffee and salad were enough for me, I hadn't expended much energy flapping my jaw with Dotty and flipping through catalog pages. I took a short nap and was awakened by a window salesman wanting to inspect my windows and replace bad ones. I told him I didn't make that type of decision and he withdrew to the sidewalk and sauntered away swinging a clipboard. I watched him for about a minute and curiously, he didn't stop at any other house on the street. He was a big burly guy and it was the first time knowing I had access to a weapon that I thought of dashing down the hall to get the revolver if he attempted to come into the house. I made sure the doors were locked and started a list of items to take with us on our Saturday expedition.

Blankets, water and food were the first three articles, then I jotted a note to make sure we charged our phones before we headed northeast on 285. I remembered that Chanel 8 had a weather report for the week at one o'clock, so I picked up the remote and turned on the television. The weather girl was talking about road closures and mentioned that 285 was closed. Using my cherished key for the first time, I went to the computer in the stamp room. I Googled a map of our area and planned our alternate route on highway 9 to Interstate 70. I estimated the distance to the city to be a bit over 100 miles. The computer stated it was 109 miles from Summit's Way to Denver but didn't designate the route. It should take us two hours, about a half hour longer than usual on 285. Frank will be happy I figured out a new path to travel. It wouldn't surprise me if Frank had already determined the route. From conversations at the post office, he probably knows that 285 is closed. He gets more news from locals than we get from newscasts on radio or TV.

I made plans for a variety of sandwiches to be made Friday evening. I didn't want food to be ageing in the refrigerator for three days. The middle of the afternoon was spent exercising Fred. He didn't want to wear his sweater, but when he was suited up, he ran to the door to go outside. We braved the cold and walked around the block. When we returned home, I checked the temperature, Thirty eight degrees Fahrenheit, not really that cold for Summit's Way considering our late December-early January temps which were typically at or below ten degrees. Fred was so happy to get back inside out of the chilly weather, he went to his bed, curled up, and went to sleep. I didn't try to remove his sweater. He'll let me know when it should come off. He won't eat dinner until it is removed. I think he's afraid to get food on his clothes.

Frank got home at six o'clock, changed into his jeans and sweatshirt and put on slippers. During dinner I brought up that 285 was closed and he said he had heard about it this morning from a customer. Then he commented we'd go by route 9 to Interstate 70. That's what I planned, but I kept quiet. He liked being the one in charge and I didn't need to take any of his thunder. We talked about items to take in the car in case we get stranded or God forbid we have an accident. The things I had earlier decided on were mentioned and Frank suggested one more item, an air pump of some sort for the tires. He'd leave it up to me to find one before Saturday.

"Oh, one more thing. Get a large package of kitty litter."

That took me by surprise. "Are we taking Blemish with us?"

"No way. I want something to use for traction in the snow."

I answered, "Okay, scented or unscented?" Then we began laughing.

"Good one, Marilee." I'll have to remember that.

The remainder of the week passed quickly as I gathered items for our trip. When Friday arrived, I piled everything together on the sofa and made six sandwiches. I ensured two empty one-gallon plastic milk containers were full of water. Just before Frank came home, I stood there looking at the assembly thinking whether I forgot anything. I decided I'd better remind him to safely package the stamps he wanted to sell. I knew he would do that and I'd probably get a dirty look but I wanted to say something so he wouldn't forget to take the expensive postage. It would be a disaster if we got to Denver and realized we didn't have the stamps.

After dinner Friday, Frank backed the car into the garage and we packed everything into the rear seat. When all our stuff was loaded, it looked like we were going on a weeklong trip into the high mountains. We stood there scanning all our belongings and I looked up at Frank, "Don't forget the stamps."

"Yeah, I've got them in a glassine envelope between two pieces of thick cardboard so they don't get bent. They're in my overcoat pocket. I'll put my coat with yours by the door so I don't forget it."

I smiled, "You would never forget your overcoat, you know you'd freeze without it."

He replied, "That's God's truth," and laughed.

"How's the gas?"

"I left the office a few minutes early and on the way home I filled the tank."

"It looks like we're ready to hit the road. Let's go inside and get ready for bed. When we get up, I'll make a big breakfast. Let's try to be on the way by nine o'clock, okay?"

"Sounds good. Remind me to weigh myself if I forget. I forgot last Tuesday. I hope we don't run into any snow on Fletcher's Pass. That pass is notorious when there is early snowfall. We'll probably see some police vehicles watching for speeders and wrecks."

CHAPTER 16

We had the house locked up like Fort Knox by 8:55 a.m. and made the turnoff to route 9 by 9:15. The road was clear, the sky gray and the two lanes had sporadic traffic. We only saw one semi and it was heading in the opposite direction. I turned on the radio, but it seemed to irritate Frank. I expected him to tell me to turn it off. He dislikes western music which was playing but he likes Dolly Parton when she appears on TV. What man doesn't? He reached over and pressed the off button.

I gave him a dirty look but he had his eyes on the road and didn't notice. We were ten miles from the pass when low spots started becoming foggy. When the pass was two miles ahead, we began to notice patches of snow along the roadside. It didn't look very deep, an inch or so, maybe two. The elevation signs indicated we were going to reach the summit at over nine thousand feet. When we passed the eight thousand foot marker, snow began to fall but only lightly. Frank didn't bother with the wipers. As we continued climbing in elevation, the snow became thicker, requiring wipers. No one seemed to catch us wanting to pass until we reached the summit, then the cars following us began to pass.

"Why does everyone on the road want to pass? We're at the speed limit and with the snow, I think I'll slow down a bit. Then every traveler on the road will want to pass. I hope no big trucks overtake us. Our wipers might have a hard time."

Frank slowed as he indicated but only a few cars wanted by. Dropping down from the summit, we relaxed when the snow let up at eight thousand feet. As the road began to clear, a car shot by us like the state police were after it. Frank commented, "Did you notice that speed demon? I believe that was the yellow car we talked about at home. I think I've seen the passenger before; it's that new deputy."

I hadn't paid that much attention but his comment piqued my interest. "Was that sexy chic driving?"

"Couldn't tell, the top was on."

"Hard top?"

"Uh-huh, didn't you see it?"

"I saw it but I don't look for things like that. I'm just wondering if the inside with a fabric top is colder than a hard top. I noticed it was white."

"I guess that depends on the heater."

"Yeah, I guess. Sometimes I wish I knew more about cars."

"You know enough, dear. You put gas in the tank and step on the pedals."

I grimaced, "You know what I mean."

We must have gone about ten miles when Frank slowed the car. I glanced at him wondering why he took his foot off the gas. "Is there something wrong?"

"Not with our car. Look over to the right in the ditch—it's that yellow car that passed us a ways back going too fast."

"Are you sure that's the same car? It's on its side. I'm not sure it's even yellow. I wonder if anyone's hurt. We'd better stop and see."

"Yeah, I was going to pull over. If my phone works, I'll call the state patrol. Get a blanket from the back seat."

We stopped on the shoulder and got out. A siren could be heard in the distance. Someone else must have already reported the accident. The wreck appeared like it had been there for some time, but that car had only passed us about ten minutes ago.

Frank led and I followed with a blanket trying not to stumble on the rocks and wet weeds down the gradual slope. It was about thirty feet to the car. Frank looked in the passenger window and said, "Two people are inside. The woman looks like she's unconscious. The guy is awake but can't seem to move. He looked at me. Maybe he's badly injured."

Frank yelled at the slightly tinted window, "Can you open the door or roll down the window?"

I could hear the passenger yell back, "My left arm is broken or my shoulder is out of joint. It's too painful to move. The seatbelt is keeping me from falling on Shannon. Is help coming? It seems to be taking an awfully long time."

Frank yelled again, "Yes. We heard a siren—probably from an ambulance. Are you warm in there? We have a blanket. Is the door unlocked?"

"No. I'll try to unlock it. Maybe I can lower the window. I'd like to cover Shannon with your blanket but I won't be able to unfold it. You can drop it in and I'll try to cover her up."

As the ambulance arrived, the siren was silenced and two people approached us, one carrying a medical box. One of the attendants asked, "Do you think the car is stable?"

Frank replied, "It looks like it's leaning against a large stump. The guy in the passenger seat is injured and the driver is unconscious. I've been trying to get him to unlock the door. He's attempting to lower the window."

"Okay. Please step back. We'll take over."

The second attendant, a slightly built woman in her late twenties, said "Could you get a couple of blankets from our truck? I need to assist my partner."

I listened to the technicians discuss the situation. The first one on the scene stated, "We can't get them out without help. Put a call out for the Breckenridge fire department, they're the closest."

The woman stepped back from the car and pulled out a cell phone. In a few seconds, she said, "No service, Neal. I'll use the truck's communication line."

That's when I made what I thought was a timely suggestion. "You know, the roof of the car can be detached. Could you get them out without help then?"

Neal looked at me and asked, "How do we release the top? Is the mechanism easy to get to?"

"I have no idea. Maybe my husband knows."

Frank returned to the scene carrying two blankets. I asked him, "Is there a way to get the hardtop off the car from the outside?" As I formed the question, I realized the top had to be released from the inside.

Frank didn't laugh and replied, "I've never been around a car with a detachable roof, but I'm sure it can only be released from the interior."

As the four of us stood there looking at the wreck, a state patrol trooper pulled up and exited his cruiser. The big guy asked, "Any injuries?"

Neal took over and explained the situation. The trooper pulled out what looked like a baton, extended it and struck the car's back window, fragmenting the glass. "There you go! See if you can get the top off now." He continued to remove bits of glass from the opening to provide safe entrance by the emergency crew.

Neal handed one of the blankets to his partner and said, "You'd better get in there, Sky, I'm a bit too big to get through that opening."

I assumed the woman's name was Skylar and watched her slither into the car without any problems. We heard some metallic noises, kind of a click and thump, and then the hardtop popped off and fell away, exposing the driver and passenger. Sky motioned for the second blanket which she carefully wrapped around the driver cushioning her head against the window. I wondered who she was.

I had never seen the passenger before either, but Frank said he was the new deputy from Summit's Way.

The trooper helped Neal place the deputy on a backboard, but the young man cried out in pain when they first tried to move him. He had to be removed to access the female who was still knocked out. Frank and I moved back about ten feet to give the two men room to maneuver the deputy. Frank stepped forward and helped Neal carry the young man to the ambulance. Sky moved to the woman and removed her seatbelt and supported her head and neck with another blanket. As her pulse was being checked I leaned closer and asked, "Is there anything I can do?"

"Sure, start talking to her—ask her questions, about anything you can think of."

I waited for a moment to see if the EMT finished taking the driver's pulse. Sky glanced at me and announced, "Her pulse is normal. She got knocked on the head from the steering wheel or the window.

See if you can get her to respond to your voice. I'd like to know if she's in pain before we try to move her."

"Do you know her name?"

"Yeah, the passenger is her brother, Ronald. He said she's his younger sister. Her name is Shannon Durham."

"Thanks, that will help." I dropped my blanket on the ground beside the car and knelt within a foot of the car. Leaning over the girl, I said, "Shannon, it's time for you to wake up. Do you hear my voice?" I've always thought I had a soothing voice; Frank has agreed. I continued, "You've been in an accident. You hit your head and were knocked out. Your brother, Ron, is all right except for a sore shoulder. I'll bet he hurt it trying to keep your pretty face from striking the windshield. What do you think?" I leaned back, took her left hand and gently rubbed it.

I saw her right false eyelash flutter and then her eyes opened in narrow slits. She blinked twice and moved her head back, lifting her chin from her chest. Her eyes opened wide and she slowly said, "Hi, Mom. What are you doing here? I think I've been in an accident on the way to Denver with Ronny."

I certainly was not her mother and wasn't sure how to act. The EMT whispered, "Humor her. You aren't her mother, are you?"

"Heavens no. I've never seen her before. I guess I should go along with it. Could you ask her brother where her mother is? She should be notified."

Shannon, covered with two blankets but still in the car, asked me, "Am I going to the hospital? I think I should be with Ronny. You should come with us, Mom. Don't you think?"

I felt an urge to tell her who I was but I didn't want to make things worse. She was obviously in a strange mental place. Could I cause mental damage by creating more anguish?

Then Shannon said, "Please don't tell Dad I've wrecked his station wagon."

"Don't you worry about that, dear. Your father will only be concerned about you and Ron, that you are both okay. The wagon can be fixed in a body shop—it can be made as good as new."

"Oh, sure. It's insured, isn't it?"

"Yes, it's insured. Don't worry about that."

Sky returned from talking with Ronald. She had me stand up so Shannon wouldn't overhear our conversation and whispered, "Her blood relatives died in 2001. Her adoptive family moved to Australia and Europe several years ago."

Understanding, I nodded, "When will you get her out of the car?"

"Another ambulance is on its way. We need more manpower to get her out without any damage to her neck and head. You'll have to step back so I can support her neck with this cervical collar."

Without question, I followed instructions and backed away from Shannon.

"Mom, are you leaving me?"

"No, dear. The medical people want to support your head and neck. Please cooperate with them."

"Okay. Is it still snowing?"

"No, it quit after we started down from the pass." I could hear a siren approaching so I informed her, "Another ambulance is coming to help get you out of the car. Are you staying warm?"

"Yes, but I have a terrible headache. Will you go to the hospital with me?"

I didn't know what to say. I glanced at Sky and she nodded. What could I say? I hadn't talked with Frank. "Yes, Shannon. I'll ride in the ambulance with you and Ron."

"Oh! Is he going, too? Is he hurt?"

"Ron hurt his shoulder. He needs an x-ray to see if there is anything broken."

"Oh, okay. How did he get hurt?"

I looked at Sky and she shook her head. I guess I would ignore that last question. Apparently Shannon doesn't realize Ron was with her in the car. The second ambulance arrived and two well-built young men approached with another backboard. I watched as the three men extracted Shannon from the car and carried her to the second emergency vehicle.

As the EMTs prepared to exit the scene, one of the men came forward, "The young woman wants her mother to ride with her. Are you her mother?"

"No, I've never seen her before, but she thinks I am. I guess her mind is a bit twisted. Do you think I should go with her? Is there room in back?"

He grinned, "No problem. You can even sit in a chair."

"Well. All right, but I need to talk with my husband." I looked around but couldn't find him. He must have been watching me because he beeped our car horn. He was waiting in the car; I'm sure it's much warmer inside.

CHAPTER 17

I waved to Frank and he pointed to the passenger door. I shook my head and went to the driver's side. He lowered the window.

"What's going on, Marilee? Let's move it and get to the city to sell the stamps and shop. We've wasted over thirty minutes at this wreck."

"Something's come up, Frank. The girl thinks I'm her mother and she wants me to ride with her to the hospital. Can you follow the ambulance? Hopefully, I'll get this straightened out on the ride. The EMTs think it's a good idea so the girl doesn't get too upset."

Frank was frowning as I mentioned the dilemma, but he said, "Well, which hospital are they taking her too? If I get lost in traffic, I want to go to the correct medical center. I'll pick you up and we can carry on with our plans."

I rushed to the ambulance and asked, "Where are you taking us?"

"Rocky Mountain General. We'd like to leave right now."

Frank had his window down and was leaning out with his left hand cupped to his ear. I yelled the destination and climbed in the vehicle. We were off immediately with siren howling, followed by a state patrol cruiser with lights flashing.

The medical truck maintained a steady speed of what I considered reasonable for the two-lane road, but when we hit the freeway, the ambulance accelerated to what I estimated to be about five to ten miles per hour over the normal speed limit. We were passing most of the traffic. The road was dry, no wet spots or snow were evident. The trip took about forty minutes. I watched the EMT check Shannon's vitals as we sped down the freeway to Denver. Shannon had her eyes closed most of the way but as the ambulance approached the medical center complex and began to slow, she began to look at me with a quizzical expression. I didn't say anything, just smiled.

I glanced out the window when we made a slow turn into a group of medical buildings. I noticed a sign as we turned: Ten minutes to Denver. I gave a questioning look at the medical technician and asked, "We're not going to Denver?"

"No, ma'am. We're delivering the patient to Lakewood Medical Center. We were radioed to transport the young woman here. They have a specialized center for brain injuries."

"Oh, that's great." I thought to myself, Frank will have fun finding me here. I might never see him again, well, at least not today. I hope he stays behind the ambulance and follows closely, otherwise . . . he'll go on to Denver, sell the stamps and start searching for me. I can picture him now, checking his phone for hospitals on Route 70.

The rig pulled into a sunken driveway sheltered by a four story light-blue concrete and tan brick building. It looked to me like we were four feet below street level. I felt the cold air as the rear doors of the ambulance opened and several men and women placed Shannon on a gurney and took her into the ER. The EMT that rode with us asked, "Do you want to accompany the patient?"

"Sure. I might be able to answer some questions about the accident. The young lady thinks I'm her mother."

The attendant helped me down from the ambulance and I followed the gurney to ER-12. In my eyes, the first ten minutes in that room were rather hectic, but I guess the staff was carrying out their normal duties for a head injury. I was asked to stand outside. I could see what was going on but I had little idea what those machines did. I recognized the monitors, so computers were hidden away behind the plastic covered apparatus or signals were being sent to a main computer center, perhaps not even at this hospital. I didn't want to bother the nurses with questions.

A nurse approached me and said, "Would you like to visit with the patient?"

I grinned and said, "Yes, I'd like to talk with her."

The nurse guided me to Shannon and asked, "I'll get you a chair so you can sit beside the bed."

"I'll stand, thank-you." I would be a 'talking head' sitting below Shannon. The nurse disappeared into the hallway.

Shannon asked, "Who are you? You rode with me in the ambulance, didn't you?"

"Yes, I was in the ambulance, I'm Marilee Neally. My husband and I were the first to stop to give assistance when you wrecked your car. You were unconscious, but when you came to, you called me Mom. The EMT and I went along with it and thought it wouldn't hurt for me to play your mother on the trip to the hospital. It appears you have regained your normal thinking. How is your headache?"

"It's not too bad. The doctors want a brain scan. That's the next thing they're going to do. I guess it's being arranged now. Do you know anything about my brother?"

"No, I'm sorry. All I know is that his left arm or shoulder was injured. I think you'd better ask about him. The medical staff won't talk to me about people that aren't family members."

A nurse entered the room and Shannon asked about her brother. The nurse left saying she would find out about him. I was thinking I was not needed any longer, but I decided to ask one question, "Shannon, why were you guys on the way to Denver?"

Shannon frowned and momentarily looked away. "I was fired from the insurance company and Ronny and I were going to the city to find me a new job. He has some friends in Denver. I guess I was going too fast in the car and we slid off the road. That's all I recall. I remember seeing you in the ambulance and wondering who you were, but I was still very sleepy, I thought maybe I was dreaming."

"I remember you giving me a strange look, but I didn't say anything. I was afraid I might make things worse."

Shannon smiled and asked, "Why were you travelling on that road? Were you and your husband also going to Denver?"

I nodded and answered, "Yes, we were going to sell some stamps to a dealer in Denver."

"You mean postage stamps?"

"Uh-huh. Frank, my husband, has some expensive stamps to sell so we can contribute to the astronomy observatory to be constructed in Summit's Way. He has a big interest in astronomy. I'm getting into it too."

I suddenly thought of Rose and wondered if Shannon had any experience with elderly souls. Maybe she could live with Rose; it might be a good fit, and Shannon might discover what her calling is. So, I had to stick my nose in her affairs.

Shannon's pretty blue eyes seemed to be drilling into me for help. I took off my heavy jacket, folded it in the middle, placed it on the chair seat and sat down. Now we were at the same eye level. "I have some questions for you. Have you gone to college or had any job training after high school?"

"Just a week at the insurance training facility. I tried sales at McDonald's but I'm allergic to the odors from the grills. I had to quit."

"How about modeling? You have a great shape for fashion modeling."

She almost started to laugh, but I could see that it hurt her head. "In Summit's Way? Maybe in Denver, but only with outer clothing. I don't like to parade around nearly naked. I guess I'm too conservative, courtesy of my parents. Ronny made that suggestion before . . . I mean about modeling. He said I'd meet some good looking men that way. But I'd like to find something to do to earn a living—something serious I enjoy doing. I'm almost ready to give up. I don't know what to do."

So, she was foundering. I had to tell her about Rose. Of course, I would have to have a heart-to-heart with Rose to see if she would entertain the idea.

"I just got an idea, Shannon. Let me explain. A really nice elderly woman in her nineties is a retired librarian and lives alone. She has been coming to my bridge club meetings the last two weeks. She's very smart and I'm thinking she could use some help around her house and moving about town. I don't know if she would want to have someone living with her, I'll have to investigate. Do you think you would like to try it?"

Shannon seemed hesitant to answer, so I suggested, "I'll let you think about it. I'll give you my number and you can get in touch if you think it's something you want to attempt. Please call me on Monday if you want to try it. By that time, I'll have talked with Rose. Of course, she might not be in favor of what I'm proposing. Will you be in Denver after getting out of the hospital? I can come pick you up if things work out."

Shannon looked around the room. "Where are my things? I don't see my phone. It's always nearby. If I can find it, I'll give you my number."

I looked for something that resembled her belongings but didn't see anything. Then my eyes came to rest on a wall cabinet marked PATIENT. I opened the door where I found a large transparent plastic bag containing shoes, a small red purse and a bright-pink telephone. She certainly wasn't afraid of color.

We exchanged numbers and a nurse appeared pushing a gurney adorned with two pillows and a blanket. "Time to get a picture of your head, dear. We have to travel down the hall, into the elevator and down to the basement." She glanced at me and asked, "Do you want to wait for Shannon? It will take about twenty minutes."

I stood and said, "No, I don't think so. I need to locate my husband."

I gripped Shannon's left hand momentarily and said, "I think you are going to be fine."

She squeezed my hand and replied, "Thank you Mrs. Neally for riding with me and being here. I'll be sure to call you unless they make me stay here for more than a day. I might still be here on Monday."

"If you're still here and you want to meet Mrs. Toliver, I know where to get you. Just give me a call." I turned and left the room to find the admissions desk, the most probable place to find Frank. I followed the exit signs down a fairly long hallway, turned left, and went through an automatic door to the admission's front desk. I had to wait in line behind two people before I could ask if Frank left me a message.

I was sitting near the hospital main entrance waiting for Marilee to arrive from the interior of the medical center emergency facilities. I was scanning through a magazine and glanced at the automatic doors when I heard them swing open for the fourth or fifth time. I saw Marilee exit from the ER entryway and walk directly to the front desk. I'm sure she didn't see me because I was partially obscured from sight behind a large concrete column.

I smiled, thinking of my next move to inform her of my presence. I placed the magazine on the bench seat and walked slowly up behind her. She didn't look around. I tapped her on the shoulder and asked, "Ma'am, would you perhaps like a ride to Denver?"

A bit surprised, she turned around and exclaimed, "Where were you? I didn't see you when I came through those automatic doors."

I pointed over to the main entrance and said, "I was sitting on a bench waiting for you to come through those motorized doors. You couldn't see me because of that big pillar. Are you ready to go?"

"Yes, I was just starting to look for you. I thought the front desk might know where you were but I guess that isn't necessary. Where's the car?"

"I parked in a visitor parking space. It's not far. Zip up your coat, it's cold out there."

We walked about fifty yards to the car. Frank opened the doors with his key remote and we got in. He started the engine to get some warmth in the interior before we got on the road about a quarter mile away from the medical complex. He waited until we were on Route 70 before asking about Shannon. I was a bit surprised he hadn't asked me about her sooner.

"So, how is the girl? Does she still think you're her mother?"

"No, she's conscious and seems in full control of her thoughts. She's got a headache though."

"That's understandable. She got a pretty hard rap on her noggin. What about her brother?"

"I don't know where he was taken. I guess he was going to be x-rayed to see what was wrong with his shoulder. I suppose he's in the same hospital. Do you think they would have taken him somewhere else?"

"I don't know. I was keeping my eyes on your ambulance and didn't see where the other one went."

"I'm sure the hospital personnel will get them back together. I mean—they *are* brother and sister."

CHAPTER 18

We arrived at Denver's city limits at noon and I suggested we find a place to eat. Frank agreed and we stopped at the first burger place we saw. There was a Chicken Palace but we ignored it and stopped at the next closest quick food place, McDonald's. We knew what to expect and it was going to be a fast in and out stop. Frank and I were interested in selling the stamps and I wanted to do a small amount of shopping before getting out of the city. I wanted to conduct our business, get back to Summit's Way and have a talk with Rose before dinner, if possible. I was anxious to discover if she would entertain the idea of having Shannon live with her. I had to think of several good reasons to try to convince her if the idea wasn't appealing.

We ordered burgers and coffee. Frank added one serving of fries; I didn't argue, I wanted them too. I figured if I only ate a salad in downtown Denver before getting back on the road home, my morning weigh-in wouldn't show any abnormal deviation. The fries were gone before the burgers. I was anticipating Frank going back for more fries, but he refrained which surprised me. Then he observed, "You've been abnormally quiet, Mar, What are you thinking about?"

"I told Shannon I would ask Rose if she could use a housemate, someone to help her navigate Summit's Way. I've noticed Rose getting very tired after our bridge club meetings. I'm fearful that one day in the near future Rose will pass away because no one is there to help her."

Frank grinned, "That housemate deal would give Shannon four make-believe grandmothers and one great-grandmother. Do you think she can handle that?"

"Well, she's kind of timid. Maybe if she associates with more women, she'll gain some confidence and maturity."

"Maturity, that's for sure. All five of you ladies are more than twice her age." He chuckled and said, "You'll have to give her some tips on building confidence. She probably lacks some observational skills, too. Has she ever had a steady job? How long was she an insurance agent, two weeks?"

"She's tried several jobs but seems to have failed in all of them. She is becoming frustrated. I think she's missing the desire to push ahead and needs some role models. She spent less than a month with the insurance job and was canned. She's going to call me on Monday if she's interested in living with Rose."

Frank mulled it over, "But you're going to be in a spot if Rose doesn't want to have a housemate and Shannon does. Then, what are you going to do?"

"I guess we'll have a houseguest for a while."

Frank gave me a menacing glare and raised his voice. "No way! We're not having that young woman staying in our house!"

I looked around, slightly embarrassed at Frank's outburst. People in the nearby booths were gazing at us probably wondering how soon the management would have us ejected from the restaurant. I didn't think we had created much of a scene—there was only a short outburst.

Using my normal voice, I uttered, "Not so loud, dear. I can hear you without yelling."

Frank scanned the neighboring booths, stood up and said, "Sorry, I didn't mean to scare anyone. I was shocked by something my wife said." He grinned, sat down and said, "Are we finished? Let's get out of here."

When we were back in the car, I asked, "Where is this stamp place? Have you been there before?"

"Yeah, I was there once. It's not too far, it's a little way off 278th, on our left."

It took us approximately fifteen minutes to find the store and a parking space. Philatelic City was in the middle of the block lit by a bright neon sign shaped like a postage stamp. The interior was a well-lighted comfortably heated room with glass display cases on all four walls. A central sales area where a bearded man about Frank's age and a slightly younger woman with green streaked hair sat on bar stools surrounded by more glass display cases. The cases were full of albums and stamp collecting accessories. I recognized most everything from seeing things in Frank's stamp room. There were several customers busily viewing the displays, mostly men, but two women were talking with the female counter attendant. One of the women was asking about new stamps from Austria.

Frank extracted the protective package from his overcoat and approached the bewhiskered gentleman. I moved closer to Frank, waited and listened.

"For a microsecond I thought you were pulling a gun from your coat." The man laughed and inquired, "How might I help you?"

Frank opened his protective package and showed the dealer the stamps. "What can you give me for this set?"

After the dealer examined the stamps, he said, "You have a nice well-centered used set of Zeps here. I'll give you twelve hundred for them if you want to sell."

Frank didn't hesitate and said, "It's a deal. I need the money."

"Okay, let me write up a bill of sale and you can sign it. I'll need your name, license and present address." He gave us a stare, "You'll swear these aren't stolen?"

"I'll sign that they aren't stolen. I've had them for five years. I bought them in Los Angeles."

Al, the dealer, filled out a form in less than a minute and handed a clipboard to Frank. I noticed the name on the form, Al Hampton, and watched Frank read the document. He signed it and gave Mr. Hampton his driver's license. When Al returned Frank's license, he asked, "Are hundreds okay with you?"

Frank said, "Sure, if they're not counterfeit," and laughed.

Al counted out twelve Benjamin notes. When I heard "twelve," they shook hands and thanked each other. As we started toward the exit, Al called out, "If you have any more like that, I'll give you a good price."

Frank stuffed the small stack of bills into his wallet as we reached the door. Frank held the door for me, but turned toward Al, smiled and replied, "Thanks, Al."

A couple of minutes later we were in the car with the heater set on high. I asked, "Did you expect that much for the stamps?"

Frank nodded and commented, "I paid a little over a thousand for them, so with inflation during the last four years, I think we came out about even. What would you like to spend two hundred on today?"

"Nothing. Let's go home. I'm already worn out. That wreck messed up my day. I'd like to talk with Rose before it's too late in the evening."

"Okay, we're off to Summit's Way. We should get home by four thirty if we don't stop for another wreck." He looked at me and smiled, shifted to drive and we were off to the freeway.

Frank seemed to know a quick way to get back on the freeway, so I sat back and closed my eyes for what I thought was a minute or two. When I opened my eyes, we were out of city traffic. I viewed the light traffic on the road going west and Frank switched to the faster lane. I checked my phone for the current time and discovered I had dozed for a mite over ten minutes.

Frank said, "You've only got a twenty-five percent chance of the deal with Rose and Shannon taking place. You know that?"

He must have been thinking about the proposal when I was asleep, calculating the odds. I thought for a moment and replied, "That's only a mathematical calculation, I think with my gift of persuasion, it's more like fifty percent."

Frank grinned, "I think my math is a better estimate of your success with Rose and Shannon than your persuasive skills. But I don't want Shannon to be living under our roof, not for one minute."

I laughed, "Oh, ye of little faith. I have been cultivating my skills over the last forty years. You don't recall how many times you have fallen under my spell."

He chuckled, "So, now you're admitting to be a witch? That's something I can't fathom. Have you been putting something in my food?"

"Yes, love and elbow grease."

We started laughing so hard that we had to wipe our eyes. Frank had me hold the steering wheel momentarily while he used his handkerchief.

I changed the subject, "How are you going to pay the thousand to the observatory guy? Will he accept a credit card?"

"No, Doctor Tyler had Ray set up an account at the bank limiting withdrawals to only funds reviewed by the construction committee. Tyler and Ray wanted to make sure no one could get their fingers in the cookie jar. I'll deposit the money at the bank on Monday."

"That sounds like a good insurance plan; it keeps everyone honest. When will concrete be poured? It's too cold now, isn't it?"

"Dr. Tyler said the winter months will be used for planning. When the ground temperature stays above freezing, the floor of the observatory will be poured, otherwise it will be too expensive. No one with low temperature concrete work experience is available close to Summit's Way. We'll have to wait until March or April to break ground. Remember, we have to determine a site first."

I didn't know much about construction projects, but I knew that Bendik's Brick and Concrete in Summit's Way had done foundations and basements for new homes. I'm sure they could handle the floor for the observatory, especially with Dr. Tyler's eagle eyes watching their every move. Ray said the doctor was a real stickler for details.

As we descended from the pass, I began to look forward to seeing the outskirts of our hometown. My watch indicated 4:43 when we entered Summit's Way city limits. We pulled into our driveway five minutes later.

Frank suggested I make some fresh coffee while he started unloading our belongings. It felt so good to stretch my legs after spending so many hours of the day riding in vehicles. When I entered the house, the first thing I did was adjust the thermostat to seventy degrees. Then I started Mr. Coffee. Frank piled our things on the sofa making two trips to the car, locked the doors and sat down at the dining room table. I could see that he was tired, so I said, "Don't close your eyes or I'll have to use a funnel and pour the coffee down your throat."

"I have to assume that's a threat. I'll stay awake for fear of the consequences." He gave me a slight grin and unbuttoned his overcoat. "Hey, you gonna call Rose?"

"Uh-huh. Would you mind if I invite her over for dinner?"

"So, that's your plan to get her to agree on having Shannon as a housemate, make Rose so grateful for dinner, she will say yes. Clever thinking, Mar."

"That's not the only reason to have her come for dinner. I thought you would like to talk more about astronomy and keep her informed about the observatory plans. Also, wouldn't you like to know if she has any knowledge about stamps? I bet she knows about the zeppelin issue."

"Good idea. I wonder if she knows Professor Tyler." He gave a big sigh, "Yeah, ask her over, but you better pick her up. I doubt if she'll want to walk over here. It'll be dark before long and without clouds it's gonna be cold tonight."

"I was going to ask you for the keys to the car. It's probably still warm inside. My car is cold and it would be a waste of gas to warm it up for such a short trip."

Frank agreed, reached into his pocket and put the keys on the table beside my coffee mug. I still had my coat on, so I grabbed the keys and started out the door. Frank called out, "Should I start anything for dinner?"

"No, don't bother. Rose and I will fix dinner when we get back."

"You're sure she'll want to come over?"

"Pretty sure. I'll be back in about twenty—with Rose."

Ten minutes later, I was in Rose's driveway. Even though it wasn't dark yet, her porch light was shining and the lights in her living room were on. I imagined her sitting in that overstuffed rocker reading a thick book. I slammed the car door to let her know a visitor had arrived and hurried to the door. I didn't need to knock; Rose met me and invited me in.

"Marilee, what brings you over this evening?"

"Frank and I want you to come to dinner. I have a big question to ask and Frank wants to talk more about the observatory—to bring you up on recent events. He also wonders if you know anything about stamp collecting. We sold some stamps to a dealer in Denver today so we could donate to the observatory fund without delving into our savings."

CHAPTER 19

"Oh, my, it's been ages since I collected stamps. I hate the new forever stamps with their sticky backing. They can't even be soaked off paper for mounting in an album and they don't have values as part of the design."

"So, you collected one time?"

"Yes, when I was much younger. I had what I thought was a nice collection of United States stamps. I didn't collect the foreign ones, but that was long ago before my first marriage. I had some good pictorial issues."

"What do you think, would you like to have dinner with Frank and me?"

"Why not? It would be fun to see his collection. My stamps are in a box somewhere—I'll have to find them. Maybe Frank can use some of them."

"You'd be his friend forever Rose. Let's go!"

I helped Rose with her coat and she secured her front door although she had some difficulty with her key. But she didn't require any assistance getting in the warm car. I drove straight home with my passenger. As we entered the driveway, I noticed Frank had taped some cutouts of bats, witches, ghosts and pumpkins on our picture window. He must have noticed our neighbors' decorations when we returned from Denver. His competitive nature forced him to react. I had to smile when I saw what he had done in the short time I had been away.

He greeted us at the kitchen door and helped divest us from our coats.

"Hi Rose, how are you?"

"Just fine, Frank. I hear you sold some stamps today in Denver. Did you get a good deal?"

"Yeah, I sold my set of zeppelins to get Marilee's and my contribution for the observatory construction. But it looks like we won't start construction until next spring."

"I understand. The cold weather is good for stamp collecting though. Perhaps after dinner you can show me some of your collection."

"I'd be glad to. I didn't know you had an interest in stamps."

"I had a collection when I was younger, actually much younger, about seventy-five years ago," she grinned. "I put it away when I discovered books and boys; that's my B and B."

We all laughed and I asked her to come in the kitchen to help with dinner. "Frank, you can watch football. Isn't there a college game on today?"

Frank took my hint and left Rose with me in the kitchen. He knew I was going to ask Rose about Shannon moving in with her. He didn't know whether I had approached the topic yet. I imagined the TV volume would be kept low.

I gave Rose a head of lettuce and she began making a salad. She made quick work of the preparation, adding some cheese strips, croutons, thin slices of carrots and some spices. She had eagles' eyes when she opened the refrigerator. I didn't have to tell her where things were located. While she worked on the salad, I made a large quantity of macaroni and cheese, almost enough for a small army squad. Frank was going to have several lunches of mac and cheese next week.

Rose and I gabbed as we assembled the components for our meal. I finally found an opportunity to mention the yellow car wreck when Rose asked about setting the table. "On our trip to Denver, Frank and I came upon a car that had gone off the road. It was the yellow one we were seeing around our neighborhood. We were going to report the accident but help was already on the way. A brother and sister were in the car, both injured. We went with them to the hospital and I talked with the driver. It was a former insurance agent, a young woman named Shannon."

Rose was listening closely as she carefully placed silverware on the dining room table. She was holding a knife when she turned and asked, "Was that young lady really an insurance agent?"

"Not anymore, she was fired. She has had several short-lived jobs and is getting frustrated searching for something she can do to earn a living. She is a bit limited because of her lack of education. I was thinking that you might help her out. Would you consider having her as a housemate? Before you react I would like to suggest that she could ferry you around town, help with things like shoveling snow and have someone for conversation. She would eliminate any loneliness that you might have. You would be a great teacher to introduce her to some real life events. Maybe you could even teach her to play bridge." I took a deep breath and waited for her reaction.

Rose gave me a momentary frown and then stated, "I don't think so. I'm happy the way things are. How old is Shannon?"

"I'm not sure but I think she's in her early twenties."

"Then I could be her great grandmother. We would have little in common."

"That's okay, Rose. I thought you might be interested. Shannon needs a place to roost for at least the winter months. Oh! By the way, her brother is Summit's Way's new deputy, so I believe she is honest."

"Well, Marilee, let me think about it."

"That's fine. I don't want to pressure you. Let's get Frank to the table and enjoy our expertly prepared cuisine." I grinned and called to Frank, "Turn off the TV, bud, we're about ready."

I had a small plastic pumpkin as a centerpiece with a candle inside. I lit the candle, had Rose take her seat, and we waited for Frank. I sat at the end of the table with Rose on my right and Frank opposite her on my left. I thought those positions would make conversation easier. Since I was a beginner in both stamp collecting and astronomy, I thought it was best that way. I would be the gofer.

Rose offered to say grace, so she thanked God and us for the meal and togetherness. Following the amen, Frank reached for the mac and cheese and passed it across to Rose. Then, he started the salad and passed it to me. I guess he was used to being at the head of the table starting the serving dishes to the right and left. It had been so long since our daughter had moved away after her marriage, I think Frank and I had almost forgotten having a third person join us for a meal. We, of course, had hosted and attended parties for postal workers and bridge club members and their families, but seldom had intimate dinners.

There were empty drinking glasses at our plates. I had forgotten to fill them with water and Frank asked for coffee instead.

Rose was satisfied with water and I got myself some tea from the refrigerator. As I filled glasses and Frank's coffee cup, I asked Rose, "When did you become interested in astronomy?"

She cocked her head up at an angle. I assumed she was thinking of how to answer.

"Gosh, that is a good question, Marilee. You're making me dredge up memories from long ago. I think I was in the sixth grade. Our science book had a photo of the Andromeda galaxy and explained all those points of light were stars like our sun. It was mystical back then."

I replied, "Andromeda galaxy?" I had never heard of it.

Frank said, "I'll show you a picture of it after dinner."

I listened to them exchange ideas for the next half-hour, occasionally inserting a question. Feeling left out, I kind of wished they were talking about bridge, something Frank knew little about.

When we finished with dessert, we followed Frank and squeezed into his stamp room. In this case, I think I was as interested as Rose. Frank had her sit at his desk and he opened his United States airmail album. I noticed the absence of the zeppelin stamps we had sold in Denver.

He informed Rose, "We sold this set today."

She moved her head closer to inspect the illustrations and commented, "I think I have two of these stamps in my collection, the two higher value ones. Do you think I could donate them to the observatory fund?"

Frank and I glanced at each other. Frank uttered, "That would be a wonderful contribution, but don't you want the money for them? If they are in good condition, they should bring about eight hundred dollars."

Rose looked up at Frank and said, "I could get a substantial deduction on my taxes then, couldn't I?"

Frank and I said in unison, "Yes, Rose." Then Frank added, "For a contribution of that amount, Dr. Tyler might have a plaque in your name mounted on the wall in the observatory. Something you would be remembered for."

Rose smiled, nodding, "I'd like that."

We looked at nearly every page of Frank's several U.S. albums before Rose announced with a yawn, "I think I should go home now, folks. I'm getting very tired. I have enjoyed our get together very much, thank you."

On my way back from Rose's, I tried to think of how to tell Shannon that Rose did not favor the housemate idea. I hadn't said another word to Rose after the initial proposal. I didn't want her to feel any pressure or cause any ill will. I began to feel bad if Shannon was agreeable to the deal. How would I tell her the housemate project was not viable?

As I went in the house, Frank met me and said, "It seems that Rose is not in favor of your plan, Mar. Sorry." He took my coat to the hall closet and asked, "Does Mr. Coffee have any more vital fluid in him?"

"Want a half-pint? I'll put some in a mug." The TV came on and I assumed Frank was going to watch the last few minutes of a game. I put enough cold coffee for two in the microwave and finished what Frank had started, rinsing off the dinner plates. I was loading silverware into the dishwasher's segmented container when the phone rang. I immediately thought it was one of my bridge buddies cancelling for Tuesday.

"Hello."

"Hi Marilee."

"Oh, hi Rose. Did you forget something?" I listened closely. I could tell from her voice that she was tired. But what she said surprised me. She had changed her mind and would like to try having a housemate. She agreed that Shannon would be a good choice, but it might be only temporary and she wouldn't be able to pay her very much during the trial period. Then Rose asked me, *"What do you think would be a fair amount for her salary?"*

I was unprepared to answer, so I called to Frank, "How much do you think Rose should pay Shannon to be a live-in companion?"

I asked Rose to wait a moment while I talked with Frank.

Frank came into the kitchen. "She changed her mind, huh? A professional caregiver would get a hundred a day but Rose should begin with say, twenty, or one hundred fifty a week, take it or leave it."

I relayed what Frank had said and Rose replied, *"Okay, I can handle that, at least for two or three months. Thank you, Marilee. See you on Tuesday. Goodbye."*

"Bye, Rose."

As I hung up, I thought now Shannon has to agree to try out being a housemate with a woman four times her age. Well, maybe two opposites will attract. I crossed my fingers hoping Shannon wants to try the arrangement. I really hope the outcome doesn't follow mathematical odds; I think human behavior doesn't depend on logic or percentages. I'd like to once say to Frank, "I told you." I smiled and considered maybe a bit of astrology can be mixed with the science of astronomy. Frank would probably be horrified if I told him that.

After we heard the third beep, Frank extracted the coffee from the countertop oven and poured our drinks. I added some artificial sweetener to mine. Frank took his straight. We sat at the table and talked for about twenty minutes. He was betting that Shannon would nix the deal; I told him he was too negative about people. He sort of agreed, having dealt with the public at different post offices for almost forty years. His memory was full of examples of strange behavior from the public.

Sunday started as usual, a late breakfast and our selective assimilation of the newspaper. We didn't pay much attention to the political ramblings, just concentrated on sports, comics, and social events. It was about two o'clock when Frank tired of professional football and went in the garage. He was out there a short time and returned with several strings of Christmas tree lights. He sat on the living room floor to untangle them.

I was looking through recipes for holiday cookies when he said, "There are only a couple of orange lights, Mar."

"Orange isn't much of a Christmas color, dear."

"Not Christmas, Halloween. I was going to put them in the front window."

I whimsically said, "Just take the white or clear ones and paint them orange." I wasn't really serious, but Frank was. The next thing I knew, Frank was putting on his coat and going to the hardware store to buy some orange paint. I hoped he wasn't going to buy a whole gallon.

CHAPTER 20

It could only have been ten minutes after Frank departed when I heard a knock on the kitchen door. There was a maroon colored Nissan SUV parked in our driveway. I wondered who it might be, none of my friends had a vehicle of that make or color. Maybe someone wanted directions. I went to the door and peered through the window. At first, I didn't recognize the woman, but suddenly I realized it was Shannon. Her presence was totally unexpected. I thought she would be in the hospital near Denver at least until Monday afternoon, maybe Tuesday. I unlocked and opened the door.

"Hi Mrs. Neally, I've come to see you about that job."

"Come in, Shannon. You've surprised me. I thought I would hear from you tomorrow and if you wanted the job, I would come get you."

Shannon looked wonderful. The last time I saw her, she had on a hospital gown and was suffering from an obviously painful headache, and a little pale. Now she looked several years younger, more like her true age, barely in her twenties. I felt she was over twenty-one but not much older.

I had her sit on the sofa and tell me what she had decided. She took off her light jacket and smiled. "I decided to take the job you talked about. Does the elderly lady want me as a housemate?"

I had been eagerly waiting an answer from Shannon ever since mentioning the prospect to Rose.

"Yes, she wants to try the housemate arrangement but she can't pay very much, at least not to start. Rose thinks $150 a week is fair to start. What do you think?"

"That's better than nothing, and I need to learn about the position. If I do a good job, maybe she will give me a raise or at least a good reference."

"That's great news. I'll call Rose. If she's not busy, we'll go over to see her. Do you want to meet her now?"

Shannon reached for her coat and answered, "Yes, I'd like to meet her and see her home. I've never known anyone that old. How should I act?"

"I think you'll be pleasantly surprised, Shannon. Rose is a very bright lady. I believe you will enjoy being with her." I thought for a moment about riding with Shannon, but she would have to bring me back, so I decided to take my car and she could follow with hers. "I've never seen your car before. Where did you get it?"

"My brother got it for me while my car's being repaired. He can't drive yet because of his injury. I drove us back to Summit's Way this morning. My car should be fixed by next week, Ronny knows the right people."

"I guess being a deputy helps, doesn't it?" She nodded, grinned and I said, "I'll take my car and you follow. I'll park at the curb and you can use Rose's driveway. When you get your sports car back, Rose will have a ball riding with you."

As I slipped my arms into my heavy coat, curiosity about highway conditions entered my thoughts and I asked, "How was the road on the way back from Denver?"

She zipped up her jacket and said, "The snow was all gone and we made a fast trip. There wasn't much traffic."

We were ready to go but as we started out the door, I thought I should alert Rose. I had assumed she would be home. Before locking the door, I called her and told her Shannon and I were coming over. She said she was eager to meet her housemate.

Shannon stayed a few car lengths behind me during the short jaunt to Rose's. I imagined their meeting and my exodus. Frank would get home with his orange paint and wonder where I had gone. An image of him arriving with two cans of paint, one orange and one black popped into my head. I laughed out loud as I got out of my car. Shannon was waiting beside her car and smiling. She inquired, "What's so funny?"

"Oh, I just had a dumb thought about my husband. It isn't important."

Shannon was a step ahead of me and knocked lightly. Rose must have noticed our arrival for the door opened immediately.

"Come in, ladies."

I watched Rose scan Shannon from head to toe then glance at me and nod. Apparently, she approved the appearance of the new arrival. We stood in the foyer and I introduced the two women. They politely shook hands and Rose said, "Take off your coats and stay a while," then she grinned and backed into the living room. She motioned for us to be seated on the sofa. Shannon removed her jacket but folded it over her left forearm.

I had to leave, so I said, "Rose, I have to get back home. Frank will wonder where I am. I didn't leave a note. You ladies don't need me here while you get acquainted, anyway. I'll see you both on Tuesday at the Sandbornes'. Sheri lives at 317 SE Aspen. Do you know where that is, Shannon?"

She thought for a second and replied, "Yes, I do. I was on Aspen two weeks before Ronny and I started to Denver. I talked to a couple in the three hundred block about insurance. They didn't sign up. I was fired the next week. I few days later, Ronny and I went off the road wrecking my car. But the way things turned out, I was lucky to have had the accident."

Rose declared, "I have a city map, Marilee. Besides, there is always Evelyn. We'll be fine."

"Okay!" I waved to them, hustled to the car and drove home. Frank was in the garage opening a small can of orange paint. It looked like it was about a pint. Approximately two dozen clear bulbs were in a soup bowl. He glanced at me and replaced the lid on the paint can.

"Where were you, Mar?"

"Shannon showed up a few minutes after you left. She agreed to try out the housemate idea, so I took her to Rose's to get them acquainted."

As Frank sorted through some drill bits, he remarked, "I must admit I'm surprised. I didn't think the arrangement had much of a chance. Well, I'm glad your plan worked out. Congratulations, I think you've done them both a good deed."

"Thank you. What are you going to do with the drill bits?"

"I'm going to drill some holes in the bottom of that plastic bottle and screw the bulbs in the holes. Then I'll dip the clear bulbs in the orange paint and let them drip-dry." He gave me a big smile and continued, "Think that will work?"

I chuckled, "Very clever, Picasso!"

"Think nothing of it, dear. I need a big success to be able to compete with you."

I shook my head and started into the house. "I'm going to bake some cookies while you do your painting project."

"Save a bite of cookie dough for me!"

I opened my mother's old recipe box and found the directions for peanut butter cookies. In place of the half-cup of granulated sugar, I added an equal quantity of no calorie substitute. I had never used that much artificial sweetener in a recipe before so I hoped the cookies would turn out okay. The dough seemed too thick, so I added a quarter cup of no fat milk and added a dozen heaping spoonfuls of the mixture to a large cookie sheet. After twelve minutes in the oven at 350 degrees, I had a dozen light brown misshapen cookies. I placed them on a rack to cool.

As that first batch of cookies was cooling, Frank came in from the garage, sniffed the air and went straight for the oversized morsels. His nose for peanut butter led the search. As he reached for one of the creations, I said, "Watch out, they're cooling. Go wash your hands and we'll each try one with coffee."

"Geez, Marilee, you're torturing me."

I grinned and asked, "Have you finished with the orange paint?"

He answered from the bathroom, "Yep, I have forty bulbs drying. They should be ready tomorrow. I'll put a string of them in the window tomorrow after work. Hey, how did Rose and Shannon get along?"

"I don't know, I came home after I introduced them."

"Well, what'll you do if Rose kicks her out?"

I started laughing. "You have become a curmudgeon, Frank. Why are you so negative about Shannon?"

He returned from the bathroom drying his hands on a large bath towel, folded it over the back of a dining chair and sat at the table. "Those cookies smell so good. Give me the biggest one you have."

I poured our coffee and gave him the smallest cookie on the rack plus a paper napkin.

"That's the biggest one?"

"Yes. I think you sniffed too many fumes from that orange paint. It has affected your vision." I grinned and took the little cookie back, replacing it with a larger one. "Now, no more about Shannon and Rose. I'll keep you advised of any changes in their relationship."

"Hey, this cookie is really good. What about calories? Will pounds show up tomorrow morning?"

"Not if you have just one instead of six. In place of sugar, I used artificial sweetener. I'm going to take Fred for a walk tomorrow. If my weigh-in is higher than today's, I'll have to walk a greater distance than once around the block. I'll adjust the calories in your lunch if you show a weight gain."

Frank swallowed the last bite of cookie and remarked, "You would think of that. You know, these cookies even make the coffee taste better."

I thought so too. I wondered if it was a result of the artificial sweetener. Then, I began to think of what Frank said. Would Rose really kick Shannon out of her house? In that case, I suppose I would be responsible for Shannon. I initially wondered how Frank would react but I had a good idea.

Monday morning flew by with the cold north wind. I turned the furnace dial up a couple of degrees and chased Fred and Blemish around for exercise. But after the morning's weigh-in result, I needed to get out of the house and walk. A check of the weather indicated the outside temp was about forty degrees and dipping, so I decided to leave Fred inside and go for a solitary walk.

I donned my thickest sweater, made sure my gloves were in my heavy coat pockets and wrapped a winter scarf around my neck. I struggled getting my arms into my coat, but short of cussing, I was finally suited up for my walk. I would go clear over to Evie's and conduct a little snooping on Rose and Shannon.

Stepping out of the house, I encountered the wind blowing my hair. I ducked back inside, found one of Fred's woolen skull caps and pulled it on. I thought of the distance to Evie's and back: more than a mile, so I grabbed an eight ounce bottle of water and heaven forbid, I put two cookies in a sandwich bag. Those were just in case items.

I didn't pause at the door, just shut and locked it and set off on my walk. I had never timed a one mile walk but I figured it would take at least an hour before I returned home; plenty of time left to start dinner. I went one block west, one south, continuing that way zigzagging to Evie's. My watch indicated it had taken only sixteen minutes but it seemed much longer, the cold wind attempting to lower my body temperature and tugging at my tailored pants. My feet were getting cold.

Turning at the last corner, I considered stopping and going back home. But then I realized nobody would recognize me in these clothes if I were seen by Evie, Rose or Shannon. As I neared Evie's, I decided to stop and say hello. At least I will get out of the wind for a few minutes before starting back. I'm anticipating the journey home will be slower— into the wind. I'll wrap my scarf around my mouth and nose.

After climbing the porch steps to Evie's front door, I took a deep breath and let the knocker do its work. After a short delay, the door opened and Evie said, "I'm sorry but we don't need new windows and my husband has already had the furnace checked."

I had to laugh and Evie recognized me immediately. "Marilee! Don't tell me you walked all the way over here?"

"Okay, I won't, but I did. Can I come in and warm up?"

She stepped back and almost jerked my right arm off pulling me into the house. "You'll freeze your butt off this afternoon. The outside temperature is dropping fast and it's supposed to freeze tonight. After you warm up, I'll drive you home."

CHAPTER 21

I thought about Evie's kind offer for little more than a second. "Thank you for the offer, but I'm out for exercise and the temperature really isn't so bad. I'm pretty well bundled up and I just need to keep moving." I hadn't bothered to unzip my coat and my legs had already recovered from the frigid wind. I felt sure I could make it home in good time, especially if I lengthened my stride.

"All right, Marilee, but remember I offered you a quick ride home." Evie looked uncomfortable, knowing I had passed on her proposal.

Before I asked her about Rose, I inquired, "What have you been doing today?"

She motioned for me to follow her to her writing desk. I guessed she wanted to show me something instead of trying to explain it. She pointed to four items and said, "Christmas cards from two years ago, last year, my notes, and cards to send this year. I'm updating my list so I won't be sending cards to bad addresses or anyone who has passed. I've lost track of several college acquaintances. They didn't send a card last year and I take them off my list if they send a card on the Internet. Do you think I'm old-fashioned?"

"Not really. Frank and I send out cards to our best friends and if someone sends an email, I usually reply with best wishes but nothing more. But I like your approach." I didn't want to initiate any unease with Evie, she had become one of my close friends. Most of my college friends' connections had vanished in the last ten years. I understood family priorities, especially now that grandchildren's activities were garnering most of their attention.

Evie went to the front picture window and pointed toward Rose's home. "Do you know if Rose has some family visitors? That car was there overnight. I'm wondering if I should check on her."

"She has a housemate, Evie. Shannon Durham is the young woman's name. I had to butt in and help make the arrangement. I thought it was a safe situation, Shannon's brother is our town's new deputy."

Evie gave me that curious, questioning look, "How did you contact this Shannon person?"

"Frank and I helped the Durhams out of a bad situation on the road to Denver. Shannon was driving and went off the road wrecking her car, that yellow sports car. We went with them to the hospital outside Denver. When she regained consciousness, she thought I was her mother, but that didn't last long. I talked with Shannon. She was looking for a new job and I suggested Rose might agree to having a live-in assistant."

"So, I guess Shannon will be coming tomorrow to our get-together?"

"I think so. Shannon will drive Rose to Sheri's . . . that'll save you from ferrying Rose."

"Nuts. I enjoyed commuting with Rose. She is so observant and talkative on those short trips. I think she likes the drives and company."

I felt like contributing a little humor to our conversation. "Has Rose ever asked you about the bank?"

"No, why?"

"I imagine she might be planning a bank job."

Evie started laughing and I joined in. Evie put her arm around my shoulders and said, "You are so funny, Marilee!"

I checked the time and stated, "I've got to head home. Thank you for the warmup time. I'll see you at Sheri's." I adjusted my scarf and Evie escorted me to the door.

"Thanks for stopping Marilee. Don't freeze your rearend off on your way home. Call me when you arrive so I know you made it safely, okay?"

"All right, I'll do that. Bye, Evie."

The door closed behind me and I was out in the wind again. It seemed much colder than before I stopped to talk with Evie, but that made perfect sense, I just left a warm house. I had walked about three blocks when I noticed the sun dropping behind dark gray, almost black clouds. Evie was correct, the temp will be dropping tonight. The next corner was a turn to the north and I stuffed my hands deeper into my pockets. I tried to lengthen my stride, but the wind was not very cooperative, so I ventured ahead at my normal pace.

When I made the turn, I noticed a car moving quite slowly about half a block behind me. The bright headlights were on, so it was impossible for me to recognize the driver. I walked past two more houses before I stopped and stared at the car. I wanted whoever it was to know I was aware of them. It stopped, holding its position. I resumed walking.

At the end of the block, I turned east and walked faster, knowing each time I made a step I was closer to home. I thought of the gun in Frank's stamp room. I imagined pointing it at a large menacing man and pulling the trigger. Could I really do it? I stopped and glanced at the car parked at the corner, waiting to turn. It was a police car; I could make out Summit's Way Police written on the side of the white cruiser.

I was relieved and continued on to the next corner. I crossed the street walking into the wind. I heard the police car engine as it pulled alongside. I stopped and faced the vehicle when I heard the command: "Stop. Identify yourself."

It was an amplified male voice coming from the car. I hesitated answering because of the wind. Could he hear me if I didn't yell? Why didn't he pull to the curb and lower the passenger window? I decided to continue walking. If this was a real stop for a pedestrian, wouldn't the blue lights start flashing? I was extremely suspicious now. It suddenly occurred to me that the police cars in Summit's Way were blue, not white. This guy was an imposter.

I looked at the homes nearest me and ran across the lawn to the one with lights on that was closest. I prayed someone was home; there was a car parked in the driveway. I banged on the door and waited for a few seconds. As soon as the door swung open, the car sped off. I watched it turn west at the next corner.

"May I help you?" a young woman carrying a baby asked.

"Oh, yes. I'm Marilee Neally. My husband runs the post office." I took a deep breath and blurted out, "A cop tried to stop me but I don't think he's a cop. Could I use your phone please?"

"Sure, come on in, it's really cold out today."

I stepped inside and unwound my scarf. I could see a phone on the wall next to a hallway. She pointed to it and said, "Do you need a phone book?"

"No, I'm just going to call my husband, thank you." The baby began to squirm and the young lady sat in a recliner. The TV was on but muted. She told me her name, Bonnie something. I didn't catch her last name. I dialed Frank's office number and got him immediately.

"This is Frank Neally. You have reached my post office number. How may I help you?"

"Frank! It's me. I was stopped by a fake policeman and took refuge in a neighbor's house. Can you come and get me?"

"What the hell is going on, Marilee? Sure, I'll come and get you. What's the address?"

I had to ask Bonnie, "What is your address?"

"This is 814 North Adams."

I repeated the address to Frank and he said, *"I'll pick you up in about fifteen minutes when the post office closes for the day. Is that all right?"*

I looked at Bonnie and asked, "Is it okay if I stay here for fifteen minutes? My husband has to close the post office before he can leave to pick me up."

Bonnie nodded and told Frank that was fine. I hung up and thanked Bonnie for the use of the phone. Then I asked her to tell me her last name, I missed it before.

"It's Day."

I thought, how could I have missed such a short name? So easy to remember, too.

"Your baby is so cute, what's her name?."

"Thank you. This little one is Erica. She's three months. I'm on leave from the hospital; I'm a nurse. Why did you come to my door? Could you explain what happened?"

I related the sequence of events about the car following me and that I ran to the nearest house where lights indicated someone was home.

"So, you think the car wasn't a police car?"

"That's correct. I'll have my husband report the incident to the real police. He knows the sheriff. I'm acquainted with one of the deputies, but he was recently injured and is probably not working now."

"I'm glad I was here to offer refuge. I'll have to tell my husband about this. But he sometimes worries when I'm home alone with the baby."

"What does your husband do?"

"He's an electrician—trained in the army. Say, can I get you a cup of coffee?"

"No . . . No thank you, I'm fine. What is your husband's name?"

Bonnie smiled, "Sun, S-U-N."

I thought Sun-Day . . . Sunday—and laughed.

Bonnie reacted, "No, it's actually Keith. We always have to make a joke with our name. I sometimes tell people Erica's name is Mon. I usually get a delayed laugh, but some people don't get it. You are very quick, you did."

Bonnie and I talked for another five minutes before there was a loud knock on the door. Bonnie was holding the baby so I went to the door. It was Frank.

"Come in so I can introduce you to Bonnie Day and her new daughter, Erica."

Frank joined me in the foyer and whispered, "Aren't we barging in and interrupting these people?"

"Come in, Mr. Neally. I want you to meet my daughter."

Bonnie stepped forward with Erica on her hip and shook hands with Frank. "Now I know who runs the post office. Do you have any cheap stamps? Anything on sale?" She grinned.

"Afraid not, just the regular price for the forever stamps. I don't set the price for stamps."

Bonnie chuckled and said, "It is nice meeting you and your wife. I'll have a good story to tell my husband tonight at dinner."

"Frank, her husband's an electrician."

"Oh, when we start work on the observatory, I'll ask for him to do the electrical work."

Bonnie gave us a puzzled look, "Observatory?"

I didn't want Frank to get started, so I said, "That's a long story, Bonnie, we'd better leave it for another time. Let's go, Frank, and let Bonnie resume what she was doing when I interrupted."

We started for the door and I hesitated, "Thank you for being so nice, Bonnie. We'll remember you." We waved goodbye, quickly shut the door and dashed to the car to get out of the blustery wind. Inside the car, Frank looked at me, smiled, and commented, "Marilee, you've got to quit getting into these oddball situations. This time with the police!"

In spite of his smile, he irritated me. "It wasn't the real police, Frank. I told you that. The guy was an imposter! Do you think I would run to an unknown residence if something wasn't wrong? Sorry I spoiled your drive home."

We were entering our driveway before Frank had anything further to say. As soon as he stopped the car, I got out, unlocked the kitchen door, went inside and shut the door. He could fix his own dinner tonight. I grabbed my bridge book, went in the bedroom, shut the door, took off my coat, scarf and stocking cap. I wadded up his cap, threw it at his closet door and watched it fall to the floor. I put on my nightgown, got in bed and started reading my bridge book.

Not more than five minutes went by when Frank knocked on the bedroom door. "Are you coming for dinner? I've heated some things so you don't have to cook. I want you to tell me the whole story of what happened this afternoon and why you were so far from home."

"Just go away, Frank, I'm not hungry. And you can sleep on the couch near your precious orange lights."

"Oh, come on Marilee. I was a bit frustrated after working all day. I'm sorry."

I didn't answer and a minute later I heard him walk away. He can play with his orange lightbulbs or his stamp collection. I wouldn't be involved with those things anyway. If I keep away from him, I won't say something I might regret. As I recounted what he said at the Days' house and on the ride home, it struck me that this was our first disagreement in a long time, maybe years. It was times like this I wished I had my own livelihood. I should have completed my senior year in business school at Oregon State. I've become a dependent housewife . . . after all those lousy part time jobs when he was in school.

After calming down, I remembered I was to call Evie when I got home. I cracked the bedroom door open and listened. Frank was in the stamp room working with the computer; I could hear the clicks of the keyboard. I was barefoot, opened the door and sneaked into the kitchen and called Evie. As soon as she answered, I whispered, "I got home okay. Bye." I returned to the bedroom and shut the door. Frank hadn't heard me or he would have said something.

CHAPTER 22

When I woke up at seven o'clock Tuesday, my first thought was to make breakfast for Frank, but I smelled coffee, so I decided not to hurry. Frank had to get ready for work, so he was probably making toast and coffee and perhaps frying an egg. I wondered if he had remembered to weigh himself. I tossed back the covers, slipped into my bathrobe and slippers and went to the bathroom. He would hear the water running and the toilet flush and know I was up. I hoped he was a bit anxious about what I would say to him after telling him to sleep on the sofa.

I planned to act like nothing had happened, I just got up a bit late. Tuesday was my bridge club day and I wasn't going to start off annoyed or agitated. I was curious to see if he had decorated the front window with his orange colored lights or had retreated to his stamp room after we got home.

Frank was sitting at the little table in the kitchen eating some cereal. He looked up when I approached. He stood up and said, "I'm sorry I caused you to be upset with me. I should have been more concerned with your situation. Please tell me what happened and why you were walking so far from home."

Frank had set the table for two, made coffee and gotten some dry cereal. I assumed he didn't want eggs, but I asked him, "Would you like some eggs? I'll tell you what happened as I scramble them."

"That's not necessary unless you want some. Sit, have some coffee and tell me your story."

I glanced in the living room as I sat across from Frank. I noticed the orange lights were around the picture window and glowing. He poured my coffee and I smiled. Overnight, Frank had become more attentive. Sleeping on the couch had apparently stimulated his thinking about our marriage. He had changed, but I wondered if his new demeanor would be permanent.

I started to tell him about wanting to walk to Evie's but I hesitated, "Won't you be late for work if I tell you the entire thing?"

"Ah, don't worry. Post Office employees can open without me for once. Tell me what happened."

The details were probably not important, but I forged ahead, leaving nothing out. I even admitted wanting to snoop on Rose and Shannon.

"When I reached their street, I wanted to get out of the cold wind for a few minutes so I went directly to Evie's. I was positive nobody would be watching out the windows for passersby and recognize me. I was so puffed up in layers, I felt like the Michelin Man. Evie offered me a ride, but I declined her taxi service and started back home. I was walking the zig-zag route. At one corner, I noticed a car that appeared to be following me but I couldn't recognize the driver."

Frank asked, "What did the guy look like? Was he big, small, skinny or fat?"

"I couldn't see in the car, the lights were on high beam and in my eyes, but that's when I realized the car was white. When it got closer, I could see Police written on the side, but Summit's Way police cars are blue, not white. When the driver ordered me to stop and identify, I ran to the nearest well-lit house and knocked on the door. The car took off when Bonnie let me in."

That was almost the whole story, the only part I omitted was the call to Frank to pick me up at the Days' residence. He knew that.

"Well, you did the right thing, Mari. That was good thinking. Did you notice the car's license?"

"If there was one, I didn't see it. I wouldn't have remembered it anyway; I was too scared. I just wanted to be with someone and safe. Oh, there was one other thing. I thought of the gun and whether I would have the nerve to shoot someone."

"You don't need to worry about pulling the trigger. You could shoot somebody if you were in danger. I'm confident of that. You don't know how tough you are." He grinned and said, "That's one of the reasons I married you, dear."

I chuckled, "Thanks, you were looking for a real live frontier woman, huh?"

"Not that, but I wanted someone that could stand her ground and take a punch." He stood up and said, "I'd better get to the office. I'm going to call Sheriff Abbott. If this is a new investigation, he will assign a deputy to look into it. Whether it is or not, he'll undoubtedly send someone over to talk to you."

He put on his coat and checked for his car keys in his pants pocket. As he opened the door he said, "There was another thing I liked about you, too. You were very sexy." Frank stepped outside but held the door open, turned and said, "Still are!"

I started laughing, waved like I was pushing him, and replied, "Go to work or you'll get fired!"

He blew me a kiss, shut the door and got in his car. I watched him back the Taurus out of our driveway and disappear down the street. Before I turned away from the door, I saw two youngsters, about fourth graders, a boy and girl, walking to the corner bus stop. The big yellow bus ferried at least two dozen kids to elementary school about a mile away. The high school was even farther, another four blocks from the grade school. I kind of missed sending a child off to school.

I locked the door and picked up the breakfast dishes. It was easy loading the few items in the washer. I put on a housedress and sneakers, read a bit of my book and started cleaning the bathroom. I hated scrubbing the toilet bowl, but if I didn't do it . . . would it ever get bad enough for Frank to react—maybe, after I was dead and buried. Well, I guess I shouldn't complain much, he keeps his stamp room and the garage spotless. And he also mows and waters the lawn. Oh, yes, he does feed the animals . . . occasionally.

The bathroom wasn't in bad shape and I finished scrubbing in about ten minutes. As I was going to sit for a minute to contemplate my wardrobe for the afternoon, the phone rang. It was Sheriff Bert Abbott asking me if I wasn't busy, a deputy would come to interview me. I said for him to go ahead. In a calm reassuring voice, he said the deputy should arrive in a few minutes. I was slightly surprised that Frank had contacted the police so quickly.

I hung up and scanned the living room to make sure it was in good order. There was nothing that would embarrass me, so I sat and waited. When I heard a car stop in the driveway, I went to the door and glanced through the little window to make sure it was a policeman. As he approached the porch, I recognized him; it was Deputy Ron Durham. His presence disturbed me. How could the sheriff allow a deputy to drive with only one hand?

I opened the door a second or two prior to his knock and said, "Hello, Ronald." Before he could utter a word, I smiled and invited him in. He was holding a clipboard in his left hand, a pen in his right. He had taken his arm out of his sling. He stepped into the living room exhibiting a slight frown that suddenly changed to a smile. "I just figured out why the sheriff grinned when he sent me over here without giving your name," he smiled more broadly.

"I recognize you. You and your husband stopped when we wrecked Shannon's car on the way to Denver. You're Mrs. Neally. I never got a chance to thank you. Thank you for your assistance. You talked with Shannon, but we were in different parts of the hospital. I didn't see you before you left."

"We were happy to give assistance. How is your arm?"

He raised his left arm to his shoulder, but from his facial expression, I could tell he was exhibiting some pain. "The x-ray showed it was out of joint and they popped it back in and gave me some pain meds. Then they taped me up like some kind of mummy and gave me this sling. The next day I was sore but able to travel. I rented a car and Shannon drove us back to Summit's Way, but I guess you know that. Thanks for helping Shannon find a job, even if it's only going to be temporary." We sat there looking at each other for a moment and then he said, "Now, what can you tell be about this recent incident?"

I related my entire experience to the deputy, even the name of Bonnie's baby. I didn't mention the thoughts I entertained about the gun. I wanted that to be a secret. Afterward, I asked, "What do your parents do, are they in law enforcement?"

"They were in one of the towers in New York on 9/11, same with Shannon's. All four of our parents were killed."

That jolted me. "But I thought you and Shannon had the same parents. You have the same last name." That's when I realized they must have been adopted by the Durham family but were not blood relatives. "Shannon must have been awfully young and you, too. I'm so sorry you lost your parents in that horrible attack."

"Thanks, Mrs. Neally. The Durham family adopted us eighteen years ago. After Shannon finished high school, the Durhams moved to Australia, but Shannon and I didn't want to go. The Durhams left us with enough money for a couple of years and then we were on our own. We stayed in contact awhile but last Christmas was the last time we heard from them. Their other children live in Europe."

So, that explained why Shannon seemed so lost and was looking for a job that meant something. At the time of 9/11, Ron, though young, wasn't affected as much as Shannon. Now I know why he entered law enforcement; at least it made perfect sense to me.

Ron stood and smoothed his pants, closed his notebook and said, "Thank you for the interview— and the help on the road Saturday. Here's my card." He gave me a blue card fished from his breast pocket. "If you think of anything else, please call me. I'll get this report to the other officers. Maybe we'll catch this guy." He nodded and asked, "Were you able to do what you desired in Denver?"

"Yes, we sold some of Frank's stamps to make a contribution to the observatory fund."

"So, your husband is a collector. He must have lots of valuable stamps."

"Only a few. He keeps them all locked in the extra bedroom, his stamp room."

"I hope everything is insured."

"Yes. Frank made sure of that."

"Okay, then, I'll let you get back to what you were doing. Bye."

"Bye, Ron." I escorted him to the door and he waved to me as he climbed into his cruiser. What a nice young man. That's when I noticed the orange lights were still shining, outlining the front window. I walked over to the outlet and pulled the plug. I glanced at my watch. It was nearly eleven o'clock, time for a quick low-cal lunch and then I'd get ready to go to Sheri's.

Tom and Sheri Sandborne live across town from the Meyers' on Aspen, which really isn't that far, less than a mile to the southeast. That was the newest city real-estate development initiated about ten years ago. There are still a few vacant lots remaining for new homes. Streets have names of trees.

Tom and Sheri graduated from architecture school at the same time but met on a project in Denver. They had been dating other people and weren't aware of each other until they were assigned to the same project. Within a year they were married, lived ten years in Denver and then tired of the city and looked for a small community.

Tom was hired as Summit's Way city architect and Sheri occasionally commuted to other cities to contribute technical knowledge and advice. Since Covid, she hadn't done any contract work. She maintains that the bridge club provided mental stimulation thus preserving her sanity.

When I arrived at Sheri's, Evie and Dotty were already there. I could tell by the cars at the curb and in the driveway. There was no sign of Rose and Shannon. Dotty answered the door and asked, "Isn't Rose coming today?"

"Didn't Evie tell you? Rose has a ride, she has a housemate, Shannon Durham. I'm sure they'll be along."

I removed my coat, scarf and gloves and stored them in Sheri's hall closet with the other gal's outerwear. Sheri was in the kitchen getting tea and coffee ready and I caught the aroma of what I positively identified as angel food cake. Sheri had gone out of her way for a treat.

CHAPTER 23

Evie and Dotty had begun the puzzle transfer from the cardboard traveling sandwich to the dining room table. I joined them and dumped the jumbled pieces in the center and around the edges of the puzzle. We began turning the inverted pieces right-side up. Two beeps from a car horn alerted us of new arrivals. Sheri announced, "That's got to be Rose and Shannon." I wasn't aware that Sheri knew about Shannon. Rose must have called ahead.

I rushed to the door and greeted the women. Shannon was steadying Rose as they stepped into the foyer. I wondered how Rose could have become unstable on her feet in such a short time. She seemed like a rock when I saw her on Saturday, a rock but slow.

Shannon stepped up to me and, in a near whisper, commented, "Rose tripped on Sunday—on a lamp cord. She hurt her hip but she wouldn't let me call a doctor. She's very stubborn."

"I understand. Let me introduce you to the others. Rose and you can sit at the dining room table for the first couple of hands. Turn over the puzzle pieces if you like."

Following introductions, Sheri informed us of the treats on the kitchen counter; we should help ourselves. Our regular group started the first hand of bridge. Sheri dealt and I was her partner chosen by picking the highest card from the deck. I picked the ace of spades so got the honor of partnering with the day's host. We called it an honor even though we all enjoyed the same ability at the game. As Sheri distributed the first hand of cards, I noticed in my peripheral vision, Shannon and Rose were flipping over puzzle pieces and talking quietly. Shannon was smiling.

Dotty and Evie won the first contract of four hearts. Sheri commented optimistically, "We'll get 'em on the next one, partner."

Dotty dealt the next hand after I had explained to the group what had occurred when I was walking home Monday afternoon. I told them the entire story and even the interview by the deputy, Shannon's brother. When I mentioned her brother, she appeared to freeze like a stone statue. I thought that behavior was strange, I would certainly be proud of having a brother as a deputy. I wondered if any of the other girls noticed Shannon's reaction.

Sheri and I bid four no trump but were one trick short of our contract. That's when I suggested we take a refreshment break. Sheri and I had to put our heads together to try to get something in the win column. I had a small piece of angel food with coffee and the snack seemed to sharpen my senses. I hoped the cake wouldn't be noticeable on my Wednesday weigh-in. I stayed on my feet as I ate the cake to burn off at least a small fraction of the calories. Sheri touched my arm to get my attention and said, "I think we all need to carry one of those pepper spray devices. Do you know where we can get them?"

I hadn't thought of the defense units before and shook my head, "I don't know but I'll bet we can get them from Amazon." I grinned, "Amazon has just about everything imaginable."

I huddled closely with Sheri for a quick review of our bidding techniques before getting back to the game. Rose and Shannon moved their chairs closer so they could watch the card play. Shannon whispered to Rose as the cards were revealed. Rose nodded to Shannon as her housemate's questions revealed she was beginning to understand the game.

As soon as our group had all dealt, we took a break and worked on the puzzle. It was coming together slowly and at the rate we were working on it, it was going to take until Thanksgiving to assemble all the pieces. We still could not tell what the picture was but there was blue sky and a few fluffy clouds in the upper half of what looked like a panoramic view. Assorted pieces for the bottom half of the picture appeared to depict roof tops of buildings. There was enough room for all six of us to work simultaneously.

Shannon held up a piece and exclaimed, "This looks like a woman's apron! I think it's a street scene, maybe part of a harbor. I'll bet it's in Europe, maybe Greece or Italy."

Dotty possessed the greatest talent for putting together puzzles. We stood away from the partially assembled picture and Dotty said, "I think Shannon's idea is correct or at least very close to what the puzzle depicts. It might be a painting. I'm wondering if it has a signature. Look for writing on some pieces as we put the bottom part together."

As we fit in the final pieces of the sky, Sheri mentioned the time. "It's almost four o'clock ladies. I think we'd better quit for today. Our next meeting will be at Dotty's home."

Dotty commented, "Let's meet a half-hour earlier—at one thirty. That will give Shannon and Rose time to play. I'm assuming they will be partners."

Rose remarked, "You ladies better be prepared, Shannon and I will make a fierce team of competitors."

Shannon surprised me, thanking us for our hospitality. As she helped Rose into her overcoat and slipped on her own heavy jacket, she turned to Sheri and nearly whispered, "The angel food cake was delicious, thank you very much."

Sheri replied, "It was nice meeting you, Shannon. Take good care of Rose, she's a real treasure." Shannon smiled and nodded.

As the youngest and the eldest women walked slowly to Shannon's rental car, the rest of us prepared the puzzle sandwich for the trip home with Dotty. After Dotty and Evie were on their way home, I assisted Sheri to rearrange her living room furniture. When we were done, She surveyed the room and said, "That's the way it was. Tom won't even know we had a meeting today."

I smiled, "Are you keeping it a secret?"

"No, that was just commentary. Everything is back in the original carpet indentations." We moved to the kitchen and I noticed about one quarter of the cake remained. She cut two thin slices and I forced myself to take one. She grinned, "I have a question for you, Marilee. What do you think of me ordering a half dozen of those handy pepper spray devices, one for each of us?"

"You know, Sheri, that's a great idea, but you don't need to pay for six, I'll do half. Okay?"

"Okay, I'll order them and you can reimburse me when they arrive. I'll buy the little ones that we can keep in our purses."

"Let me know when you get them. I'd like to be armed—just in case I'm out walking."

When I got home, I was met at the door by Blemish and Fred. I think they had grown tired of the noiseless house and wondered where I had gone. After giving the pets some love, I turned on the TV with the remote. The five o'clock news from Denver was just beginning. As I put away my things in the hall closet, I heard the weather report from the east coast, almost always the first item on the national news and usually about Route 95.

Local weather came after the west coast summary. The mountain states hardly ever ranked first unless there was a disaster of some kind. Frustrated with the news coverage, I went to the kitchen and started a fresh pot of coffee. I felt a bit embarrassed when the first thing after coffee that came to mind was angel food cake. I had to laugh when I considered slapping my face.

As the news was ending, the phone rang. The handset display said Raymond Meyers but it was Evie.

"Hi, Evie! What's cookin'?"

"I suddenly had an idea and thought I'd run it past you—see what you think."

She had my attention; I muted the TV sound so nothing was competing for my hearing. "What are you thinking?"

"Why don't we all get those pepper spray units, we'd have a defensive weapon against that guy that tried to stop you on the street."

I was unsure how to respond but I had to say something or Evie would wonder why I was silent. I chuckled, "Great minds come up with the same ideas! Sheri and I just ordered a half dozen of the pepper spray devices from Amazon. We'll hand them out to everyone next Tuesday at Dotty's place. I'll tell Sheri you came up with the same idea. Won't it be great to have something with us for protection?"

"Exactly! I'm glad that you and Sheri don't think it's a foolish idea. It came to me because Ray has all the tellers at the bank provided with pepper spray." She paused for several seconds and whispered, *"Oops, don't tell anyone I told you that."* She giggled, *"Ray told me to keep it under my bonnet."*

"Don't worry, it's our secret. I won't tell Frank or the other gals."

"Well, I guess that's all I had to say. Don't go out on any more long walks until you have some protection."

"I won't, Evie. I just heard Frank drive in the garage. I'd better go. Bye."

"Ray will be home from the bank before long. I'd better start dinner. Bye Marilee."

I put the phone in the wall cradle and met Frank at the door, unlocking it so he didn't have to use his key.

As soon as he came in the kitchen, he remarked, "Is that some new perfume or is that fresh coffee I smell?" He tilted his head back and sniffed, then shrugged out of his overcoat and gave me a kiss. "How was your bridge club meeting today? Did you win?"

"We didn't complete a full game, but Shannon and Rose seemed to be getting along fine. We worked on the puzzle, too. We have an idea that it might be a picture of a painting. I told them all about the fake cop and taking refuge at the Days' home. We've decided to order pepper spray so we have some protection from strangers."

"Pepper spray, was that your notion?"

"Nope. Sheri and Evie came up with it. I believe it's a good idea, don't you think?"

"Yeah, I guess so. It least it's not lethal. That would prevent shooting yourselves if you had guns, too. Ray said they have all the teller locations at the bank equipped with the spray. It should at least slow down any robbers."

"Ray told you that! He made Evie swear not to let it out of the bag."

"It's no big secret, Marilee. Don't pour the coffee yet, I need to change my clothes." As he walked down the hall to the bedroom he asked, "What's for dinner?"

I raised my voice so I was sure he heard me, "Leftovers. Should I order some pizza or chicken?"

"No pizza. That will ruin our weight loss program."

I grinned, "How about ordering a small one?"

"No pizza!"

"Okay! We're having reheated spaghetti and meatballs with some wine." I was kidding about the wine but he didn't say no. I decided to have some fresh salad and coffee to go with warmed over spaghetti. The salad only took a few minutes to prepare before Frank returned to the kitchen.

He sat down and queried, "Did someone go in the stamp room today?"

"Was the door unlocked?"

"Uh-huh. My U.S. definitive album was opened to the 1938 presidential series. I don't remember doing that. Was anyone here today?"

"Oh, yes. I forgot to tell you. Shannon's brother, the new deputy, Ron Durham, was here to interview me about that encounter with the fake policeman. Ron was here for about a half hour. We had a good talk. I told him on Saturday we were on our way to Denver to sell those stamps. We had to stop and help at the wreck. He asked if your collection was insured."

"I'm a bit surprised that the deputy was on active duty. What about his left arm, was it in a cast or a sling?"

"No, he said they put it back in joint and taped him up like a mummy."

"You're sure it wasn't a daddy?"

I had to chuckle, "Very funny Frank, you must have had a good day at the post office."

"So, the deputy didn't go near the stamp room?"

"Nope. We were in the living room the entire time. He didn't hypnotize me either."

"How would you know, Mari? I must have gone in there last night and forgotten."

I guess he had me there. "Come on, enough about the deputy's visit. Let's have a quiet dinner and then you can work on your stamps while I read. You can turn on those orange lights, too. I kind of like them. They're getting me in the mood for Halloween. I'll have to stock up on candy next week."

"Well, please keep the treats away from me."

"I noticed you forgot to weigh yourself again."

"Yeah, I'll try harder to remember in the mornings. Maybe I'll put one of those sticky notes on my clean underwear."

"Now that's sure a good idea. Right on the crotch of your shorts."

CHAPTER 24

The week passed in agonizing fashion, the days dragging by. The only thing interesting was the up and down of the daily temperatures, quite cold one day and warm the next. Although when I say warm, I should say warmer than the day before. On Friday, Sheri called to tell me the pepper spray devices had arrived. There was one call to ask me if we wanted to sell our time share. Wherever they got the idea Frank and I had a time share, I have no concept.

Sunday's local paper, *Summit's Way Views*, contained an article from the local police blotter. Apparently a twelve year old girl had been approached by a man disguised as a policeman, but she was suspicious and ran from him. Fortunately, she was only a few houses from her home and nothing happened. The youngster's suspicions arose because the man was driving a jeep, not a police car. The following writeup also reported an older woman had been approached earlier in the week. I assumed that was about my encounter and report. The police were of the opinion that the suspect was dressed in a Halloween costume masquerading as a police officer.

I told Frank I was pleased that no names were given. He teased me saying, "They should have mentioned your name so you can say you had your name in the paper. All your card playing friends would be envious."

"Oh, pfft! Would you want your name in the paper if someone broke in and took your stamp collection?"

"No, I guess you're right not wanting your name printed."

Frank folded the paper over to the sports section but there wasn't much there except a few high school football scores. The social news didn't exist but there was a note about a new restaurant opening in another month. Perhaps the owners are hoping to get a good start before Thanksgiving. It was my opinion that they should wait until spring or summer when the weather was better. But what did I know, maybe they will deliver. If so, Frank and I will have to try them out—we rarely go out to eat.

Frank wanted pancakes for breakfast and I was looking forward to them too. I bought a bottle of low calorie syrup to get away from the regular stuff that's loaded with calories. I'd heard that there was an ingredient in the restricted diet syrup that gave some people gas, so that was not something to look forward to, although Frank would enjoy the experience. He loved beans for the same reason. He remembered something from high school about beans being a musical fruit but it was not something I wanted to repeat if I could recall the words.

The temperature in the afternoon rose to about forty-five, so we took Fred for a walk. We didn't notice any strange vehicular traffic, in fact, the streets where we walked were almost barren. If there weren't cars in driveways, one would think no one lived in the adjacent neighborhoods. Fred wore his cold weather walking gear. After going only three blocks, we returned home. His wagging tail indicated he was happy to get back in the warm house. So was Frank.

Frank turned on the orange lights as soon as the sun began to dim. He ventured outside briefly to look at the glowing bulbs. When he came inside, he said, "I'm gonna take a look at the moon and Saturn tonight, the sky is supposed to be clear."

I shook my head and commented, "You'll freeze your patoot tonight, dear, the temp is going to be below thirty-two."

"I know, but there aren't going to be many days until spring when I can observe the moon and a couple of planets. I'm sunk if it's cloudy."

"Okay. I'll make some hot chocolate so you can thaw out after."

"That's a great idea, thanks. Maybe some popcorn too, without butter?"

Frank had kept his coat on and took his telescope outside to equilibrate with the exterior temperature. I smiled when I imagined him sticking his tongue to the freezing cold telescope eyepiece. I decided to keep some warm water handy just in case. Fortunately, the eyepiece detaches from the telescope, so he could come inside without carrying the entire telescope if the eyepiece gets stuck to his tongue. As soon as I visualized the concept, I relegated the idea to being a passing fancy, it would never happen.

After dinner, Frank went into the backyard and focused on the moon after inserting the appropriate filter. I was in the kitchen preparing the dishwasher for another run when I heard Frank call, "Marilee, put on your coat and come outside. You've got to see this."

I thought I'd better do what Frank requested or I'd never hear the end of it. I wondered what he had seen on the moon. I just hoped it would live up to the enthusiasm and urgency expressed in his voice. I put on my heavy coat, wrapped my scarf around my neck to lessen any exposure and joined him. When I bent down and looked into the telescope eyepiece I saw a small striped ball and four nearby stars.

I queried, "That's Jupiter and four stars?"

"You're partly right, dear. That's Jupiter and the four Galilean satellites—not stars but planetary moons. Pretty cool, huh?"

I had to admit I was glad he called me out to see the display. I posed a question, "What will that look like in the larger telescope in the observatory?"

"Jupiter will be much bigger with more detail of the cloud bands. We'll be able to take some cool pictures, too."

"My fingers are freezing, Frank; I'm going back inside. The hot chocolate will be ready when you come in."

"Okay, I'm going to take one last look before I come in. I'm going to put the scope in the garage."

Monday started off to be just another day but Frank came home for lunch with some disturbing information. The eldest member of the post office staff, Rosy Cooper, related the story of her granddaughter, the twelve-year-old that had run from the man in the jeep. I had to smile when Frank said, "Rosy wants to cut off the guy's family jewels when they catch him. She wants to use a box cutter and make him eat them."

I had an image of the shackled guy sitting at a prison table being served with his own Rocky Mountain oysters. I seem to be haunted with these ridiculous images. I wondered what my brain would concoct next. I didn't mention what I was thinking to Frank; he would think I was ready for the loony bin. However, I seemed obsessed the entire afternoon with hatred for this guy that was harassing older women and young girls. Just what was he up to? I could think of rape, torture and murder. I hoped the police would mount some type of search for this deviant.

I didn't sleep well Monday night. I couldn't get that girl and her grandmother out of my thoughts. Maybe a day with my girlfriends would settle my frustration with the acts of this weirdo. I could only hope the police would catch this guy before he did something unforgiveable.

Higgins' residence was about the same distance as Evie and Ray's but to the east on Mayhill Drive. Mayhill was one of the founding fathers of Summit's Way and the first mayor in 1883. He was killed in a gunfight in 1891. He wasn't even involved in the argument; a stray bullet ended his life.

I arrived at 1:25. Sheri was the last one to show up and only a couple of minutes late. She had an excuse; she was actually ten minutes early but forgot the pepper spray devices and had to return home to get the package shipped by Amazon.

We didn't want to start anything without her, so we were gabbing when she arrived. She placed the package on the bridge table and we watched closely as Rose did the honors and opened the small shipping box. Each unit was packaged separately and Shannon gave them out.

Rose grinned, "Should we draw cards to see who is selected to test the first spray?"

Sheri reacted, "I don't think we want to do that, Rose."

Rose laughed, "I wasn't serious; it was a joke." We all laughed.

Evie voiced an opinion. "I've been thinking of something but I would like your viewpoint."

Our voices hushed. Evie had everyone's attention.

"I believe everybody saw the article in the paper about the guy imitating a policeman. And now we know from Marilee that the girl that was being lured was the granddaughter of one of Frank's post office workers. Can we do anything about this guy?"

Rose raised her hand.

"Yes, Rose."

"In olden times, before there were sheriffs, marshals or police, townsfolk volunteers would form a vigilance committee. I think we've all read about them or seen such groups in western movies and TV."

Dotty exclaimed, "We could be vigilantes!"

Sheri was a bit subdued, "So we catch this guy and string him up?"

Dotty added, "Yeah, by the testicles."

I laughed, thinking of my mind's eye from the day before. Everyone looked at me, so I said, "We cut off his nuts and make him eat them."

Dotty added, "Raw or cooked?" Everyone giggled.

Evie remarked, "Let's get serious, ladies. If we form a vigilante group, we have to develop a plan of attack. But first, are we all in favor of doing it?" Evie polled the others and received nods or "Yeses" from everyone. "Okay, then, who will be our leader?"

Rose suggested, "Marilee has been the person involved with both reported incidents, so I suggest she be our leader."

I had never been the leader of anything before. I considered refusing, but then I thought maybe I should break the mold and try something new. Frank could always give me advice and none of the women except Rose knew I possessed a gun. I wondered if that was the reason Rose nominated me.

None of the other girls spoke up but I had an inkling Evie wanted to be in charge since Ray was the bigwig of all the husbands. I hoped she would exhibit no ill will. I stated, "Does anyone else want to lead the group? If not, shall we have a silent vote?"

I was surprised when Evie suggested, "I think we should consider acclamation. All those in favor say aye." A chorus of ayes ensued.

No opposition was voiced. I didn't notice if anyone failed to vote. So, that was it. I said, "Let's play bridge for an hour and then we'll see if anyone has a plan to apprehend this pervert."

In the second hand I was dummy, so I picked up an extra score sheet and drew lines representing the route from Evie's to my house, the way I had walked previously when the imposter stopped me. The sketch resembled a stairway. How was I going to devise a safe way for us to monitor a decoy walking along the streets?

Dotty noticed my drawing motions and asked, "What are you scribbling, Marilee?"

"I'm trying to figure out a foolproof method to catch a bad boy—something we can all take part in." Dotty smiled and played a card. I decided to make a list of our woman power, vehicles, etc.

Number 1: six women

Number 2: five drivers

I didn't know if Rose could drive a car. I had to ask her. Rose and Shannon were working on the puzzle, but the hand ended and I couldn't lodge my question. I had to bid; I had four aces and a queen. Evie played the hand at five no trump; we could only lose two tricks. That gave me a chance to talk with Rose.

I sauntered over to the dining room table where Rose and Shannon were searching for a specific puzzle piece to complete a cobblestone walkway. I waited a few seconds before I squeaked out my question, "Rose, can you drive a car?"

She was so engrossed with searching for the puzzle piece, she didn't look up. "I quit driving twenty years ago, Marilee. I don't have a license anymore and the new car dash displays befuddle me. That's one reason I have Shannon." She looked up and grinned. "Why do you ask?"

"I'm working out a plan to catch that pervert, that's all. Thanks, Rose." I heard a puzzle piece snap into position.

"Got it! That was a hard one to find, Shannon."

Shannon commented, "We saw it at the same time."

I returned to the bridge table where Evie announced, "We lost two tricks to kings, Marilee."

"Sorry I didn't help you play the cards but I had to ask Rose something."

She laughed and replied, "That's okay, I was able to reach across the table—long arms you know." Dotty was next to deal and Evie said, "Let's sit out this next hand and let Rose and Shannon play." As she got up and moved closer to me, she whispered, "I've got to pee."

"Okay, I'll be at the puzzle."

CHAPTER 25

When Evie joined me at the puzzle table, I grinned and asked, "Did you wash your hands?"

Fortunately, she chuckled and pretended to slap my face. "Yes, and I used lots of soap and warm water. Dotty has a charming bathroom, it's nicely decorated. I sneaked a peek in her medicine cabinet and she has a great variety of lotions and creams."

I was surprised Evie told me what she had done. I didn't expect a confession from her. I wanted to get down to business so I showed her my sketch and asked for her input. "The little circles are car positions and the squiggly lines are for repositioning. What do you think?"

She studied my crude drawing for a minute and then remarked, "I think it's too complicated, Mari. I also think we should have a way to communicate—like with phones."

I knew phones wouldn't be a good idea. Half the time reception around town is bad or non-existent. I reminded her about the phones and she said, "Yes, but I was thinking of walkie-talkies. You know, like the ones kids use."

I must have given her a dumb look, cause she giggled and said, "You didn't think I knew about walkie talkies, huh? My neighborhood gang used them for playing army and spies. Do you know if they are still made?"

I shook my head and commented, "No, I haven't seen those things in years. Let's check tomorrow at All Sports Inc. They should know where we can get them. I think hunters use them. We can check the Net, too."

"Okay, I'll come over to your place and we can go from there. Is one o'clock okay?"

"That's good. If Frank has lunch at home, he'll be on his way back to the post office by then. Let's work out a routine for car movement tonight. We can go over the proposed locations tomorrow. I'll try to come up with a simpler scheme than this one."

"Me too."

Frank called me at eleven o'clock on Wednesday and asked me to prepare a salad, he would bring something for lunch. I could only guess at what he had planned, chicken or burgers. It would be a big surprise if it were anything else. Frank arrived with a sack of burgers, no fries. We each ate one and I put the other two in the freezer. Our chit-chat revolved around the weather and whether it was going to be a cold day for trick-or-treaters. I asked him to bring home some candy to hand out to Saturday's visitors.

"Okay, but I'm not going to splurge. If we have anything left over, we'll donate it to the hospital or the bank. They'll give that stuff away. I don't want it at the post office."

"Why not the post office?"

"Cause I'm there to sneak sweets." He grinned and I chuckled. He finished his coffee, gave me a smooch, slipped on his coat and was out the door at 12:50. I heard his car pull away.

I expected Evie in a few minutes. She was normally right on time to bridge club meetings so, that's what I expected. I decided to turn on Frank's orange lights and ask Evie what she thought of them as a Halloween decoration. As I leaned down to plug them in the wall socket near the floor, I heard her car enter the driveway. The car door slammed and I yelled, "Come on in, Evie. The door's unlocked."

As I went into the bedroom to get my favorite four-color ink pen and my sketches, I said, "I'll be right with you. Pour yourself some coffee, I made extra for lunch."

I heard a chair being scooted across the floor when I started down the hall toward the kitchen. As I crossed the rug in the living room, I could see Evie's shoulder. She was wearing a new or different coat, a camouflage variety. Ray must have bought it for her, she wouldn't have purchased a jacket like that herself.

When I came through the door into in the kitchen, I was shocked. I stopped dead in my tracks. I couldn't speak. Someone was sitting there wearing a Halloween mask of a pirate. It wasn't Evie; whoever it was, the body was way too large to be Evie. It was a man. His big hairy right hand was holding a large hunting knife. With his left hand, he was setting down a coffee cup.

In a gruff voice he uttered, "Good joe. Take a seat."

I couldn't move.

"I said take a seat!"

I winced but pulled out a chair and sat down. I couldn't keep from staring at that ugly mask. That's when I heard another car stop out front. It had to be Evie. She had to park at the curb, the driveway was occupied and she wouldn't want to block another car from exiting.

The guy stood up, went to the kitchen window and parted the curtains. He glanced at me after a quick look out the window and asked, "Who's expected?"

"A friend of mine. We're working on a project today."

"Tell her to go away."

"That won't work, we have an appointment for one o'clock. We have important work at that time."

"Okay. Get her in here. No funny stuff."

I could only hope Evie had her pepper spray unit on her key chain. That would solve our immediate problem. I went to the door with the pirate behind me. I could feel the edge of his knife against my back. What did this guy want? I had less than twenty dollars in my purse and the two rolls of pennies next to the scale made another dollar. Maybe Evie had some cash.

I opened the door for Evie and said, "Hi, Evie, come in."

The pirate stepped back pulling me with him. Evie came in and stated, "I didn't know you had company, Marilee. Who's behind the mask?"

"He just arrived a few minutes ago. I heard a car and thought it was you, so I invited him in."

"Okay, that's enough! Keep your mouths shut!"

Evie frowned, but otherwise didn't seem to exhibit any fear. I noticed she was aware of the knife.

The intruder said, "Take me to your husband's stamp collection. I know he has some valuable stamps. As soon as I get what I want, you can carry on with your little meeting."

So that was what he wanted—Frank's expensive stamps. As far as I knew, we just sold Frank's most valuable stamps. I decided to keep my mouth shut, just as this guy insisted. Evie stepped next to me, grabbed my right hand with her left, and we watched the guy rip the telephone off the wall.

I started across the living room moving slowly and said, "His stamps are in our little nursey. There's no room for three people in there, only two. Evie can come in with me."

"You're joking, of course. Evie and I are staying in the hall, you go in and get the stamps. If you try anything, Evie's blood will be staining your carpet and you will join her with lots more bleeding."

"Okay, but I don't know what stamps you're seeking. I'm not a collector. Tell me what to look for."

"I'm sure he owns a penny black, maybe more than one. That's what I've heard about. Find the album for British stamps and bring it to me.

I almost smiled; the gun was in the slipcase for British stamps. I figured I could put my hand inside the case after I extracted it from the wall shelf. I would turn to my left as I put my right hand on the gun and hold the case with my left hand. He would have to reach out to get it and I would shoot him, right through the slipcase. Frank won't care. I just have to be sure Evie's not in the way.

I had to think of a way to get his knife away from Evie. I know, I'll pretend the case is very heavy. Maybe he'll tell Evie to help me carry the album and slipcase. I pretended to be looking for the album.

"Well, get the damn album and bring it to me. Hurry up!"

I traced over the shelf of albums with my right index finger until I came to the Great Britain slipcase. I pulled it off the shelf and stuck my hand in the case following my plan. I had my back to him so he couldn't see my hands. I let the protective box sag in my arms and said, "It's quite heavy, can Evie help me?"

We were frozen in place for a moment. I hoped he was thinking. Then, I feigned a bit of a stumble as I moved toward the door. He shoved Evie through the doorway saying, "Give her a hand, bitch." He stood there but dropped the knife down to his waist. Evie was directly between us, so I whispered, "Quick, crouch down."

When Evie dropped to her knees and was clear, I pulled the trigger, "Click." Nothing happened. The gun didn't fire!

He raised the knife and lunged toward me so I pulled the trigger again. The back of the slipcase blew off and the pirate stood there looking at me. He acted like nothing happened, so I pulled the trigger again. The shots weren't too loud, I guess they were muffled by the gun being fired inside the box. I could feel the gun recoil though and the case fell to the floor. The guy staggered against the wall and sagged to the floor. He didn't say a word.

I yelled at Evie, "Go next door and call the cops . . . and an ambulance! The lady's name is Frances, hurry!" Evie ran to the front door and left it ajar when she vanished.

What should I do? The pirate looked like he was dead but he was face down and I didn't have the nerve to touch him or feel for a pulse. I don't know where I shot him but I'm sure it was with two bullets somewhere in the chest. We were too close to each other for me to miss. I wanted to rip off that mask to see what he looked like but I didn't want to get any closer. He gave off a terrible odor.

What if he wasn't dead and reached out and grabbed me? That's when I kicked the knife down the hall toward the living room to get it out of reach. I wondered if he was dead. I still had one bullet, or maybe the gun was empty if that first pull on the trigger hadn't caused a bullet to fire.

My heart was racing. I had to sit down. I went into the kitchen, put the gun in the refrigerator, and poured myself a cup of coffee. I felt a bit woozy and sat down at the kitchen table. I guess I just had to wait for Evie to come back. Maybe I'll hear a police siren or the sounds of an ambulance. I took a sip.

Cold coffee is terrible. I felt like throwing up when I realized I might have killed that masked guy. Frank is going to be disturbed about the attempted theft of his stamps. But I don't think he ever had a penny black. He didn't have an album for British stamps, just that slipcase and it was empty—except for the gun.

I heard someone at the door. I yelled, "It's open!"

"Marilee? It's me, Evie. I'm coming in. Don't shoot me."

"Don't worry, I put the gun in the fridge. I'm in the kitchen. Come and sit with me. Did you get the cops?"

Evie joined me and said, "Yes, the cops are on their way. They said they would send an ambulance. They wanted to know who was hurt. I told them a guy wearing a pirate mask and carrying a big knife." She tilted her head and remarked, "I can hear a siren."

"Would you like some coffee? It's cold. I'll make some more. Maybe the cops will want some."

"Can I ask you a question?"

I was pouring water into Mr. Coffee, enough to make twelve cups. As I added a filter and the coffee, I said, "You can ask me anything, Evie. You're my best friend."

"Where did you get that gun?"

I smiled, "That's kind of a long story. It was in that scale I bought at the antique store. Remember, you thought the scale was a person at first."

She frowned and then replied, "Oh yes, I remember. I told Ray and we laughed."

"Well, please don't tell anyone else. Rose, Frank, you and I are the only ones that know about the weapon."

Evie reached across the little table and gripped my hands. "Marilee, this will be in the paper, so everyone will know you and Frank have a handgun. It won't be a secret for long. It will be in the next edition of the newspaper unless the sheriff can keep it quiet."

"I guess you're right. I'll have to request that he keep it a private matter."

"Sheriff Abbott is a good guy, Marilee. Ray speaks very highly of him."

I nodded. "Frank says he's a good guy, too."

CHAPTER 26

Evie and I sat there for about a minute, maybe longer, time seemed to be creeping before the police arrived. Evie recognized Sheriff Abbott when he appeared at the kitchen door. He knocked lightly before turning the knob and poking his head through the opening.

"Mrs. Neally? I hear you shot someone."

"Come in. Yes, he's on the floor in the hallway. I shot him twice. Oh! The gun's in the refrigerator."

Another officer appeared at the front door. On his heels was a middle aged woman in a gray uniform. I assumed she was the ambulance driver. Following them was a slightly younger man, I guessed he was an EMT or maybe a doctor. He was carrying a small black suitcase.

Sheriff Abbott didn't say a word. He pointed toward the stamp room. A deputy and the guy with the suitcase ambled down the hall.

Less than a minute passed and a male voice called out, "Sheriff, this guy's deceased."

Abbott moved to the hall and asked, "Does the intruder have any ID?"

"Nothing on him but he might be the guy on the report from Denver about the stolen car. I ran the licenses on the cars when I arrived and one's the stolen Ford. I'm wondering why he showed up in Summit's Way."

"Do you recognize him?"

"Nah, never seen him before, Sheriff; probably homeless, BO is staggering; hasn't shaved in a long time."

Sheriff Abbott asked me, "Have you called your husband?"

"No." I pointed at the wall where the phone wires were dangling and the phone was on the floor.

"He did that?"

I nodded. "Could you please call my husband?"

Evie then asked, "Sheriff, could you call Ray at the bank? He'll want to know if I'm all right. He knew I was coming over to see Marilee this afternoon."

"Sure. I'll put in a relay call from my car to the dispatcher. Give me a minute, I'll be right back." Abbott did an about face and went out the front door avoiding the gurney as the uniformed woman pushed the wheeled metal stretcher through the opening.

The deputy was standing in the middle of the living room glancing down the hallway at the gurney. I asked him, "Can Evie and I go out in the garage?" I didn't want to see the dead guy hauled off. I feared the images would remain in my brain for a long time. The shooting through the slipcase was over in an instant and hadn't seemed to have made any indelible memories. I did remember pulling the trigger. I could still feel the gun in my hand, I guess it was like an amputee's phantom limb pain.

Evie almost whispered, "Good idea, Mari. I hope I don't have a bad dream tonight."

Deputy Hammond replied, "Sure, but don't walk off. Sheriff Abbott will want to question both of you."

I don't believe the deputy understood that I belonged in this house; where would I wander off to? The sheriff returned and had Evie and me come in and sit at the dining room table. He pulled out a small handheld recorder and said, "Mrs. Neally, I want you to tell me about your entire day—from the very start. You can stop when Mrs. Meyers joined you. Don't leave anything out. By the way, I'm noticing some bowls for pets. Where are they?"

"We have a cat and a dog, but when visitors come inside they hide under our bed. They'll come out when all the strangers leave or hunger gets to them."

Sheriff Abbott nodded and prompted me, "Okay, begin when you got up this morning."

It didn't take long for me to retrace my day's activities. When I got to the point of Evie's arrival, and my asking her to come in, I looked at the sheriff and started to tremble. I had actually asked that guy in! Then, I remembered Evie showing up and seeing that angry looking knife. The sheriff stopped me. He shut off his recorder.

"Okay, let's take a short break. I just heard a car drive up. It's probably your husband."

Frank burst into the kitchen and engulfed me in his arms. "Thank God, you're all right. Were you attacked?"

He had me in a bear hug and I was still shaking. He walked me to the kitchen table and we sat down. "Who was the guy that came in?"

"I . . . I . . . don't know." I took a deep breath, "He wanted some stamps—he said penny blacks. He had heard you had several."

"That's odd, I don't have any penny blacks. Who gave him that idea? How did you get the gun, dear?"

"I didn't know about penny blacks, so he told me they are from Great Britain. That's when I remembered the Great Britain slipcase had the gun in it. The robber, Evie, and I went down the hall and I told him the room was small and we couldn't all go in. He held the knife to Evie's throat and told me to get the album. That was his last order. I pretended the binder was heavy and he pushed Evie toward me to help. I whispered for Evie to duck down and I pulled the trigger, but the gun didn't fire. I pulled the trigger again and I shot him. He moved toward me, so I shot him again. He crumbled to the floor. I wanted to pull off his mask, but I was too scared; I was afraid he might grab me. Oh, Frank—I ruined your slipcase."

Frank smiled and held me tighter. "You did fine, Mari. To hell with the slipcase. Where's the gun?"

I pointed at the refrigerator.

He looked over my shoulder. "I don't see it."

I must have given him a strange expression, so I explained, "I put it in the refrigerator. I don't know why." I quit shaking, took a deep breath, glanced at the sheriff and asked, "Should we continue now?"

"That won't be necessary, Mrs. Neally. I recorded the conversation between you and your husband. I figured you would tell him exactly what occurred." Sheriff Abbott grinned and asked Evie, "Is that the same thing you experienced, Mrs. Meyers?"

"Yes sir. That guy really scared me. I thought he would cut my throat at any minute. I had no idea Marilee had a gun, but when he pushed me and she told me to get down, I did what she said. Then I heard a click, and then two bangs. I didn't see what happened, I was on my knees; I just heard the noises. The guy fell face down in the hallway."

There was a sudden commotion at the front door and Ray came rushing into the living room. When he saw us all grouped around the kitchen table with the sheriff, he exhaled and said, "Evie! You're all right! Thank God. When I heard there was a shooting at Frank and Marilee's house, I prayed you weren't hurt. Then I figured after the experience Marilee had on the street, she bought a gun and accidentally shot Frank. When I drove up, I saw the ambulance crew hauling away a body, but the form was too small to be Frank. So, who shot who?"

Evie grabbed Ray's arm and pulled him into the living room where they began a subdued conversation. I was glad Evie diverted Ray away from me. I didn't want to go through another explanation of the shooting. I just wanted everyone to leave the house so I could return to a somewhat normal afternoon with my book and animals. But I needed to talk with Evie.

I watched Ray depart and Evie approach me. "Marilee, I'm going home. Can we meet again tomorrow?"

I couldn't recall having anything planned for Thursday so I replied, "Sure. Things should be calmed down by then. I'll call you if something comes up."

"Okay, Mari, I'll be here promptly at one." She grinned, "Keep the door locked." Then she gave Frank a serious glance, "Take care of her Frank, she's a valuable item." Evie exited from the kitchen door. Frank and I watched Ray's and Evie's cars drive off.

The sheriff had reappeared at the front door and stated, "I'll contact you, Mrs. Neally, when I get the perp's ID and the coroner's report. I don't think there will be anything else for you to do. Try to get back to your normal activities—relax and read a book."

Frank called out, "Sheriff, should our gun be registered?"

He replied, "There are no registration laws in Colorado for handguns but keep it in the house. Find a good hiding place like you had before. What you did was clever—it worked out well."

When the sheriff closed the front door, Frank and I were alone— finally. We sat at the kitchen table and had some fresh coffee. I leaned back in my chair and asked, "Would you please check to see if there is any blood on the hallway rug outside the stamp room doorway."

He jumped up and rushed across the living room to the hall. A few seconds later, Frank called to me, "I don't see anything, Mari, but there is a slight smell of disinfectant. The ambulance people must have cleaned up." He returned to the table, exhibiting a big grin. I could tell he wasn't going to reveal any thoughts without my asking.

"Okay, what's so funny?"

"Oh, it occurred to me that when the coffee was made, we should have told the sheriff we didn't have any donuts."

I shook my head and commented, "Frank, you're bad. Would you really have said that?"

"Probably not, considering the serious nature of the police visit."

"Sit with me, dear. I just had an idea. Let's go out to eat tonight— to heck with the diet. I want to get out of the house. Let's feed the animals and go to a real restaurant. But no burgers for dinner."

I didn't have to persuade Frank to have an evening out. Before he sat down he fished his billfold out of his back pocket. He opened his wallet, checked for his credit cards and cash. He was ready to go. He took a sip of coffee and I got up. He started to get up but I said, "Stay there until I feed Fred and Blemish. Then we'll go."

The only classy place to eat in Summit's View is Conner's Restaurant on the other side of town about a quarter of a mile from where Sheri and Tom Sandborne live. Sheri told me they go there for dinner about once a month. She said the restaurant is located on a hill and the lights of Summit's Way are pretty at night. The food is delicious but it's expensive. Knowing Conner's was a classy place, I had to change my clothes.

Frank was already dressed appropriately in his suit and tie. So, right after feeding our pets, I scooted into the bedroom, changed, went to the bathroom and checked my makeup. Then I reentered the bedroom, opened the top dresser drawer where my handbags were and grabbed the nice black one with silver decorations, the one Frank gave me last Christmas.

When we were in the car, Frank let out a big sigh, started the engine and we were off for a new experience. As we passed Sheri's home, Frank asked, "Exactly where is this place located? I don't see any signs. I thought it was on Alpine."

"No, Frank, it's on Aspen. Just keep on going straight. We cross a county road and the restaurant is on the right. Evie told me we'll see the building on a hill at the outskirts of town."

"Marilee, do we need a reservation? Should I have called ahead?"

"Not according to Sheri. It's rarely more than half full."

"I'll bet it's hard to find a seat on a weekend. Ah, there it is." Frank pulled into the parking area and stopped next to the sidewalk leading to the front entrance. Even though the sun hadn't set, the walkway lights were on, a very classy look. As we got out of the car, Frank asked me, "Why did you put the gun in the refrigerator?"

"You just thought of that?" I shook my head and said, "I had the gun in my hand when I went in the kitchen and I figured I should put it somewhere no one would pick it up until the sheriff arrived. I didn't think much about it."

"Okay. I was wondering how that came about. Let's get inside and find a seat. I want to see what's on the menu."

As we entered the glass enclosed vestibule, a couple in embroidered white shirts and black pants greeted us. The male asked, "Is your reservation for two?"

Frank and I were taken by surprise and hesitated. Frank started to open his mouth when the woman gave the man a head slap and said, "Stop that nonsense, Paul. These fine people don't need a reservation. Please follow me and I'll seat you. Would you like to sit at a window or be closer to the center?"

I didn't want to freeze as I ate dinner, so I said, "Center, please."

CHAPTER 27

As we were being seated, Frank commented to the woman, "For a moment, I thought your husband was serious about a reservation."

"Oh, Paul's not my husband, he's my brother. He's an established jokester, likes to see how people react. If he weren't a one third owner, I'd fire him. We don't have reservations unless the dinner is for a celebration. You know, birthdays, weddings, that sort of thing."

She gave us each a menu and departed for about thirty seconds, returning with glasses of ice water. "Would you like to order now or should I give you a few minutes."

Frank was studying the bill of fare, but I was ready. I replied, "Please give us a couple of minutes. We're on a diet and don't want to overdo."

"That's fine. I'll seat some other guests and then return."

As she walked toward the entrance, I saw Meyers come in. "Look Frank, it's Evie and Ray. Should we ask them to join us?"

Frank grinned, "Why not, we can ask him about his bear rug."

"God, Frank, don't bring that up. That will stimulate him to ask about the shooting. Ask him about developments with the observatory."

Frank stood up, waved to Ray and Evie and motioned for them to join us. Ray acknowledged with a wave and guided Evie toward our table. Mrs. Conner scurried around them to a table for four and motioned for us to relocate.

We had an enjoyable dinner with the Meyers, talking about sundry topics—everything but the afternoon's altercation. Ray insisted on footing the bill and after a slight disagreement, Frank agreed, only if he could pay the tip. Ray said it was their thanks for me saving Evie from getting knifed. That was the only reference made to the attempted robbery. As we left the restaurant, we encountered a cold breeze, and hastily entered our cars, Evie called to me, "See you tomorrow at one o'clock, Marilee."

Frank and I arrived at home around eight o'clock, plenty of time for us to sit quietly and watch a TV movie. I scanned the channels to find something without terror or gunplay. We finally settled on a rom-com on the Hallmark channel. Ninety minutes and a dozen commercials later we began preparing for bed. I almost fell asleep brushing my teeth.

Frank weighed himself in the morning without a reminder. He didn't mention the shooting and after breakfast told me we would select a new location for the gun tonight. He'd buy some new ammunition, too. For now, we'll keep the gun in the refrigerator. I remarked that I wanted to put it in one of the two bottom drawers next to the apples.

"Will you please put the gun next to the fruit drawer?" I didn't even want to handle it. "I had a dream last night about shooting a friend and was being sentenced for murder. I woke up in a sweat and had difficulty going back to sleep."

"Sure. It'll be out of sight. Don't think about it anymore. While I'm at work, I'll think of another location for it."

I thought that would be the end of my epic involvement, but after Frank left for the post office, I must have checked the doors every ten minutes until I realized what I was doing. I settled my mind by playing with the animals for a few minutes and then found where I left off in my bridge book and sat down to read. I heard a sharp noise from the ceiling and imagined someone or an animal was trying to get in. I paused reading and listened intently. I was reminded that Frank once told me that rafters or beams in the attic would make snapping sounds sometimes when they expand or contract. I resumed reading and finished the chapter without any further agitation. I put the book on the coffee table and closed my eyes for a minute.

The minute became more than an hour. I was startled awake by the phone ringing. I blinked my eyes and figured out where I was and what time of day it was, got up and answered the phone on the third ring. It was some woman conducting a survey. I didn't want to be asked about the southern border problem so I hung up, hoping I wouldn't receive a call back. The hope angel didn't hear me, the phone rang again, but it was the same number. I let it ring . . . five times!

I went to the fridge and got the makings for a salad, got a can of soup from the cupboard, some saltine crackers and I was prepared. I snacked on the crackers as I readied the salad and soup, the only sounds were from the cutting knife and the boiling of the clam chowder. I was enjoying the solitude. The action to make sure the doors were locked didn't reoccur.

As I consumed my lunch, I worked on a leapfrog method of moving our cars, four of them, to always keep our decoy in sight, both in front and from behind. When I was tidying up the kitchen, the doorbell rang. I hadn't heard a car drive up, so I checked to see if Evie had arrived. I had to laugh when she stuck out her tongue.

We talked about Conner's restaurant for a couple of minutes before we got down to business. I had prepared tea. I knew Evie liked tea better than coffee, so we moved to the kitchen table and got out our sketches. I asked Evie to go first, thinking her plan might be significantly better than mine.

While I listened to her voice and watched Evie's pencil point to her drawing, I realized we had the same plan. When she finished, I smiled and said, "Okay, here is what I devised." I didn't say anything but showed her my sketches. Her expression morphed from a frown to a big grin, "Marilee, your proposal is identical to mine!"

We had a big giggle and decided to diagram the movements and placements of the cars on a blank sheet of paper I retrieved from the stamp room. I supplied a ruler and we drew a network of half inch squares as city blocks. Using colored ink, we marked the routes each car would take so there would always be two pairs of eyes on our decoy walker. Early on, we decided to use the path from Evie's to my house, the way I had walked previously when accosted. We also reasoned it was a good course of travel because we were all familiar with the connecting neighborhoods.

When our directional map was complete, Evie said, "What about the walkie-talkies?"

"Geez, I completely forgot about them. I'll get the local phone book and we can make some calls."

There were three stores in Summit's Way that carried the little phone systems. The ones at the hunters' supply store were too expensive, so we opted to go to Kids' Corner downtown and check out a set of walkie talkies for children. That might be what we wanted and when finished with them, we could donate to the hospital so children could play with them. Evie and I got in her car and drove to the store.

We explained the reason for the communication devices to a fairly young and cooperative female clerk. She feared for her eleven-year-old daughter and wanted to assist with our plan to catch the offender. We ended up purchasing four walkie talkies for sixty dollars. The clerk included an extra set of batteries at no charge. She wished us good luck as we left the store.

Evie and I took the children's communication units to Evie's and tried them out with one of us walking around the block talking to our buddy stationed in the living room. All the devices worked admirably, as if the government had equipped a SEAL team with them for black ops. With the devices and the car route diagrams completed, we were prepared for our next bridge club/vigilante meeting. Confident our plan was going to have a successful outcome; we imagined the creep locked behind bars.

There was one minor problem. Our scheme was devised assuming our guinea pig was going to walk from Evie's to my house and not the reverse. The next bridge club meeting was slated for my house. Evie made a quick suggestion, "Let's call Dotty, Sheri, and Rose and tell them to meet us here. We'll just switch our routine this one time."

That was the simplest solution, so we made three phone calls. I told Dotty not to bother with the puzzle, we wouldn't have time for it. She could transport it to my place for the following meeting. Everyone would meet at Evie's on Tuesday at one o'clock and activate our scheme.   After making the phone calls, Evie and I sat on bar stools at her kitchen counter drinking coffee. We talked over the plan and tried to think of problems that might arise. I thought of one, "What if our sacrificial lamb makes the entire trip without any contact with the perp?"

Evie chuckled and responded quickly, "We'll return to my house for a short break after the matinee and then do a repeat performance."

"Why did you laugh?"

"Your use of the word perp. Where did you come up with that?"

"I saw a crime drama the other day and thought everyone used the term. It's short for perpetrator. Sheriff Abbott used perp too."

Evie smiled, "Yes, Marilee. It's common slang. You surprised me, I didn't expect it from you."

I grinned, "I guess we all have hidden talents."

Friday was an ordinary day until after lunch. Frank called at eleven thirty to tell me he was going to eat at the office. I had to warn him about calories, it was my duty. He told me he had already thought of the diet and would be a good boy. At exactly 1:30, Sheriff Abbott called and told me the man behind the mask was wanted in Denver for several crimes. Until he showed up in Summit's Way he hadn't stolen any cars. The car belonged to a stamp collector that parked in the lot behind Philatelic City and accidentally left the keys in the ignition.

The wanted guy's name was Henry Floyd Garrot. He was dishonorably discharged from the army three years ago for drug addiction and drunkenness. Hank had no family and had been adopted when he was eleven. His adoptive family moved to Indonesia, but as a young adult he elected to stay behind. He entered the army to keep from going to jail. He visited stamp dealers and gathered information about his victims.

When the sheriff concluded, I asked, "Where will the body go?"

Sheriff Abbott remarked, "*The city will put him in a pauper's grave. That's cheaper than a cremation.*"

I thanked the sheriff for the information and spent almost a half hour of the afternoon thinking about the unfortunate life the criminal had experienced. I wondered how different his life might have been if he had been raised by his own loving family. Or perhaps nothing would have been altered, he still would have been killed in a different robbery. No matter what I did during the remainder of the afternoon, I couldn't keep those thoughts from invading my brain.

Saturday was rainy and windy, guaranteeing an altogether dismal twenty four hours. After lunch, I left to pick up some Halloween candy. Sunday was Halloween. Frank and I had about two dozen trick-or-treaters Sunday evening, most of them coming after dark, the little ones with their parents and the older ones in what seemed like boisterous marauding groups. However, we didn't find any graffiti on our walls or other damage to the house when we checked Monday morning. Mailboxes along the curb were still upright.

Tuesday was our V-day. Our vigilante group met at Evie's house. Everyone was present except Rose. Shannon came across the street to tell us Rose wasn't feeling well, but Rose told her to help us anyway she could. We practiced for about ten minutes with the miniature radios and made sure everyone possessed pepper spray, our chief defensive weapon.

We were all seated in the living room and I stood to ask for a volunteer to be the decoy. I think all of us older people were surprised when Shannon volunteered. She said, "I was on the girl's track team in high school and can probably outrun all of you ladies, don't you think?"

Dotty acknowledged, "The last time I remember running was about thirty years ago when Dale chased me with the hose. I threw some dirt on our car after he had just washed it. I don't remember why I did that. I must have been sore at him for something he had done, maybe an off color remark. I'm sure Shannon can outrun me."

There weren't any other comments, so we accepted Shannon as our volunteer sacrificial lamb. We swore to watch as she advanced and react to any suspicious activity, especially from occupants of cars that tried to intervene with her progress toward my house.

CHAPTER 28

The sun was out, the sky clear, but a chilly northern breeze was going to make Shannon's walk less than enjoyable. We made sure she was dressed appropriately, donned our coats, checked our radios and pepper units, and tried to think of anything we might have forgotten.

Sheri spoke up, "Let's go in alphabetical order: Dotty's first, second is Evie, then Marilee, and I'll be last for the first round. Then we'll start over. Is that all right?"

The rest of us nodded and we went to our cars. Shannon would start walking after waiting a couple of minutes for us to take our assigned places.

Shannon had traversed four blocks when we started the second round. No problems had arisen, our plan was operating like clockwork. Evie alerted us at the beginning of the second round and I was almost ready to go to Shannon's aid when I heard Evie say, "False alarm. It was a woman driver that slowed down to turn in her driveway."

I decided to turn on the engine and use the heater to warm my legs. I watched Shannon in my rearview mirror as she approached the corner. When she passed by, I noticed what I thought was a grin, but she didn't look at me, just as instructed, as if I weren't present. As soon as she was in Sheri's view, I drove to my next position, a few blocks from my house. Sheri would be waiting for her at my place, to pick her up and return to Evie's.

However, Dotty sounded an abrupt alarm. Shannon had stopped and was talking to the driver of a pink sports car. My walkie talkie squawked, "Go! Converge on Dotty! Shannon's being forced into a sports car!" I could hear engines coming to life in the sounds from my miniature mobile radio. We were on the move to rescue Shannon.

When I arrived at the scene, Dotty was parked behind the pink car and Evie's SUV was nose to nose with the soft covered convertible. I stopped less than a foot away from the driver's side to block an escape and pin the guy in the car. There was no way out for this creep unless he crawled out the passenger door. I put the car in park and turned off the engine, exited as quickly as I could with my pepper spray ready to squirt him in the face.

As the three of us approached, Shannon opened the passenger door, stepped out and yelled, "Ladies! It's okay, he's my brother! Put the pepper away. He's driving my car—he had it repainted pink. Look, it has my license plate."

As I moved toward the rear of the sports car, Sheri drove up and rushed to see why we were standing around. I called to her, "It's okay, he's Shannon's brother."

I glanced at the license plate. Sure enough, it was TUF STUF, Shannon's license. I got back in my car and pulled forward beside Evie's car. As I joined the group on the sidewalk, I recognized Ron, Shannon's brother. The sling he had worn was gone and he had his right arm around his sister's shoulders. He was explaining the new paint job to Shannon, Evie and Dotty.

He noticed me and said, "Hello, Mrs. Neally. I've been hearing a lot about you from my sister and how you arranged for her to live with Mrs. Toliver. Thank you for the help."

"You're welcome, Ron. I guess your shoulder has healed without complications."

Ron lifted his arm and rotated it, then smiled and stated, "Good as new. Still a little sore." He pointed at the car and asked me, "What do you think about the change in color from yellow to pink?"

"I like it. What about the hard top?"

"I decided to get rid of it. It was damaged anyway. Shannon can't handle it herself. The cloth top is better." He moved over beside me and said, "Shannon and the other ladies were just telling me what they were up to. We caught the guy you were planning on apprehending. He's in jail—wanted in Denver. He tried to kidnap a high school girl but her boyfriend and some of his buddies tracked him down and forced him to leave the city before the police nabbed him. Unfortunately, he came to Summit's Way to cause more trouble. He's a psychopath. I'm glad we got him off our streets."

I looked at the group and said, "I guess we should all go back to Evie's. Maybe we can play some bridge before the afternoon is gone."

Shannon remarked, "I'll take Ron to his apartment and meet you at Evie's. But first, I need to check on Rose. Okay?"

I had to smile as Shannon reached out to her brother to get the keys to her car. I think she was anticipating the excitement of driving her repaired bright pink sports car. I wondered how she was going to return the loaner. Maybe Ron would take care of it.

We dispersed to our cars to return to the starting point, Evie's house. She backed away from the front of Shannon's car and squeezed past my car. I think she wanted to get home first so no one would have to wait for her to open her front door. I drove around the block and headed to Evie's. I didn't see what the others' return trip involved. When I got back to the Meyers', I checked the time. It was only a few minutes until two-thirty. Our venture to catch the molester had taken about an hour.

We gathered in Evie's living room and were having coffee when Rose arrived accompanied by Shannon. We were pleased to see Rose. She must have felt overwhelmed by the attention, for she grasped Shannon's arm to steady herself. Shannon helped Rose walk to the dining table. They turned two chairs around so they could join in our conversation. I must admit Rose appeared a bit peaked. She must have really wanted our companionship, even though not feeling well. I didn't think she would want to play bridge today, just watch.

Sheri asked us, "What should we do with the walkie-talkies and the spray units?"

Dotty reacted, "I don't know about you guys, but I'm gonna keep my pepper sprayer."

The rest of us responded with "Me too," so that was decided. Rose spoke up about the walkie-talkies. "What about giving those little devices to the Girl Scouts? They could use them when they're selling cookies, don't you think?"

We all agreed with Rose's suggestion. Dotty responded that she knew the mother of a girl scout she could contact. We gave our walkie-talkies and extra batteries to Dotty who would take care of the donation.

I noticed Rose was scanning the room apparently searching for something. I asked, "Are you looking for something, Rose?"

"Yes. Where is the puzzle? Have you completed the picture?"

I replied, "No, we haven't finished with it. I think we have about fifty to sixty pieces remaining. We'll finish it next week at my place."

A big smile grew out of her previous tired expression. "Oh, that is good news. I want to see the final picture. It has been a long time."

Her last statement took me by surprise. I thought Rose didn't know what the puzzle depicted, but maybe my assumption was wrong. Could it have been that she assembled, or partially assembled the puzzle before? She just told us she didn't have a picture of the puzzle for our reference.

We played four hands of bridge before we decided it was enough for the afternoon. I think we all noticed Rose was tiring and probably wanted to go home to rest. Shannon assisted Rose with her coat and scarf, donned her own winter coat and they were out the door and crossing the street before any of the rest of us were wearing our winter garb.

I noticed Evie glancing at her watch as Dotty and Sheri ambled out the front door to their cars. I was the last to leave after taking a few minutes to help Evie straighten out her living room furniture. Evie remarked as I left, "I've got dinner to get ready for Ray. He said he would be home early. Thanks for helping, Marilee."

"You're welcome. See you next Tuesday."

The sky had become uniformly gray and a cold northern breeze had strengthened while we were in Evie's home playing bridge. I knew it was the harbinger of snow, not unusual for the first week of November in Summit's Way. But the cold winter weather in the fall didn't prevent us from relishing the beauty of the mountains. I imagined at least six inches to a foot of the white stuff by next Tuesday, perhaps our last meeting until the roads were cleared. Frank and I, joined by neighbors, worked to clear paths from garages to the street after the city plows piled mountains of snow across approaches to garages.

As I turned into our driveway, I pressed the remote on the visor to open the garage door.

I chuckled as I thought of Frank's proposal to put his and hers markers above the entries. I talked him out of the idea. Blemish and Fred were waiting for me as I entered into the kitchen. They were both excited and I figured they would like to go outside for a few minutes, despite the cold. They followed me to the slider and ran into the backyard when the porch door opening was wide enough for them to squeeze through.

Fred ran to the nearest tree for relief, but Blemish just sat motionless for a few seconds, looked up at me, and came back inside, as I expected. She disliked anything resembling cold weather. A short time later, I heard scratches coming from her litter box. Then noises emanated from the vertical blinds at the living room picture window. Blemish was happy to watch the outdoor activity but chose to remain in the indoor warmth. If she could find a family to take her, she would travel to Southern California or Florida, but she was well taken care of. I've always wondered how Blemish ever arrived in Summit's Way. Frank and I wondered how she turned up at the animal shelter.

Frank got home a few minutes after six o'clock, changed clothes and joined me in the kitchen. We enjoyed about ten minutes of conversation before the tuna casserole was ready.

Frank asked, "Did you hear that the cop impersonator was caught?"

"Uh-huh. Shannon's brother, Ron, told us this afternoon."

"Oh, where did you see him?"

It wasn't a secret, so I told Frank about the bridge club's plan to help apprehend the culprit. When I told him of the pepper spray units and the walkie-talkies, his eyebrows could have knocked his hat off if he had one on. He was totally surprised, even shocked that the bridge club and Shannon had carried out such a scheme. When I told him about the pink sports car, he laughed and slapped his thigh saying, "You gals had a good plan, I wish I had been there to see you carry it out. I would have liked to see Ron's expression when your cars pinned his vehicle against the curb."

"Shannon's car, dear."

"Whatever. At least you had a good time. Wasn't today a bridge club day? How'd that turn out?"

"We played about an hour. Rose came over but she was a little sickly. She did ask about the puzzle though."

"Yeah, how's that going? Is it about finished?"

"It's getting there. I think we have about fifty pieces to go. It's a picture of a street in a small town adjacent to a bay. I think it's in Italy or Greece."

"Kind of like one of those travel postcards?"

"Uh-huh, like that."

The oven timer sounded and we sat down to dinner.

After eating, Frank leaned back in his chair and announced, "I've thought of a place for the gun. Short of tearing the house apart, no one will ever find it."

I sat there looking at his confident expression. What could he have thought of? "Do I get a hint?"

"Okay. It's near where it was at the very beginning."

I mulled that hint crumb over for a few seconds and tried to picture a spot in the hallway or the bathroom but couldn't imagine a good hiding place that was also easily accessible. I finally gave up, "All right, where is it going to be? Will you put it in a plastic bag and submerse it in the toilet tank?"

"I'll give you one more hint. It will be close to water but it will never get wet."

"Above the ceiling tiles?"

"Not even close."

I started laughing and said, "Okay, you've got me. Put it wherever and I'll try to find it."

"Now that's a good idea. You'll have to give me a few minutes for preparation."

"While you do your thing, I'll load the dishwasher and launder some clothes."

CHAPTER 29

It took about fifteen minutes before Frank came into the kitchen where I was inspecting the cupboards for vacancies so I could add items to my shopping list. I carried out the process about once a month. I put down my list and watched Frank toss that short little fat handle screwdriver in the utility drawer. That stubby little tool reminded me of one of Frank's golf balls sitting on a tee. When he dropped it in the drawer, I noticed his right hand knuckles were red. He must have been working in a tight space. Another clue for me.

"Would you like a cup of coffee or chocolate?"

"I don't know. Chocolate will add to my weight and coffee will keep me up."

"I'll make some coffee half-and-half—half regular and half decaf. How about that?"

"Yeah, and some of that fake sugar," he grinned.

After we finished our drinks, Frank commented, "I should have chosen chocolate. Let's not do that coffee concoction again. It's more than half bad."

"Oh, come on, it wasn't that bad. You'll sleep like a baby."

"Sure, and I might have to wear a diaper." He looked at me to see how I reacted but I said, "Let's go in the bathroom and I'll search for the gun. I bet I can find it." While I was working in the kitchen, I think I figured out where Frank concealed the gun. I paid close attention to Frank's clues.

I put our dirty cups in the sink, walked a few steps down the hallway and entered the bathroom. I pretended to take my time, but after a few seconds of surveying the counter and bathtub, I dropped to my hands and knees and opened the cabinet doors beneath the sink. I reached below the countertop between the sink and the counter front and felt for the gun. I was sure it was there, so I slid my hand sidewise searching for the firearm. Nothing. I was so sure it was there but I didn't even encounter a spider web.

I exhaled, a little disgusted, and Frank helped me to my feet. I looked at him and shook my head, "I was convinced I had it figured out. Where is it? Is it in the bathroom?"

"Yes, it's in here. Pull out the bottom drawer, the deep one."

I followed his direction and removed the drawer from the cabinet and set it beside the sink. I pointed at the cabinet void. "You put it in there?"

He shook his head, "Not in the cabinet, under the drawer. Lift it up and feel underneath."

I tilted the drawer and looked at the bottom. There it was, wrapped in a sandwich bag and taped to the bottom of the drawer. All I would have to do is pull it from the drawer and unzip the plastic bag. I didn't bother to try it.

I glanced at Frank, "It's in a sandwich bag?"

"To prevent rusting. This room can be very humid from baths and showers."

That made perfect sense. Frank took the drawer and replaced it in the cabinet opening.

"What do you think? Is it a good place?"

I thought for a second and said, "Uh-huh. I'll run to the bathroom, lock myself in, get the gun, sit on the toilet and wait for an intruder to break down the door." My summary caused Frank to laugh and I couldn't prevent a chuckle.

Frank stopped laughing and I expected something from him, almost profound but then he grinned, "If you are in the bathroom and the door is closed, I'll be sure to knock and announce myself."

What could I say? I nodded my approval and uttered, "Fun time is over, dear; I'm going to bed."

I was busy during the remainder of the week spending money at grocery stores. Thanksgiving was not far off and I put in a request for a twenty pound turkey at Jimmy's Market. I could pick up the frozen bird three days before the holiday. I marked the kitchen calendar. We were always running short on bread and I decided to make croutons following an online recipe. I bought two extra loaves on Thursday so I wouldn't come up short right before the festive day.

Friday was an interesting day. I delivered Frank a box lunch at the post office to keep him from buying a burger and fries. When I got home, the phone was ringing as I stepped inside. I answered on what I thought was the third ring.

"Hello. Oh, hi Dotty. I just got home from the post office. What's on your mind?"

"Could I bring the puzzle over today? I might not make our get together on Tuesday. Dale has a big meeting for auto dealers in Denver this weekend and it might extend into next week. I'll be going with him; it's a paid vacation of sorts."

"Sure, bring it over. You can help me put away groceries," I giggled. "I'll set up a card table for it, my dining table is being used right now. I'll see you in a few minutes. Drive into the garage where Frank parks."

"Okay, be there in ten minutes."

I hung up the phone and started storing the goodies from my recent buying trip, cans, bottles and plastic packs of items from the morning's purchases. Our cupboards might be sagging when I finish placing everything in empty spaces. As I worked, I imagined the next time I would be doing this was in January.

Dotty's arrival in the garage was signaled with a beep from her car horn that momentarily scared me. I jumped when I heard the sound, but then relaxed, knowing who it was. As I opened the door, a sudden vision came to mind, a large figure wearing a pirate's mask. I shook the image from my mind and let Dotty in with the puzzle. I was happy to see a known face without a mask.

Dotty carried the puzzle sandwich to the card table and gently laid it down. She started to take off her coat and hesitated, "Oh, would you get the box of pieces from my car? It's on the front seat." I went to her car, the big red one. The way she parked would surely prevent the garage door from closing. That huge car was a real tank. She and Dale will be very safe on the road to Denver, only a semi hitting them would cause any damage. I grabbed the box and went back inside.

"I can't believe the size of your car, Dotty. It's enormous!"

She laughed, "We're taking it so we can return with two months of groceries, similar to what you've been doing. Dale likes to have at least eight weeks of food on hand—just to be prepared for winter storms and power outages. I think it's a little much, though. When we get back, he plans on getting two cords of wood for our stove in the basement. Cooking on our woodburning stove is a bit tricky though. The top of the stove gets extremely hot."

Dotty's information was interesting but Frank and I don't have a basement or a woodburning stove. We have, however, popped popcorn in our fireplace fires. I suppose we could try cooking other things but only in emergency situations. Ideas of making coffee and warming cans of soup came immediately to mind.

I helped Dotty unwrap the puzzle from the layers of cardboard and straighten the edges of the nearly complete scene of irregularly shaped puzzle parts. We stood there trying to imagine what the blank sections would reveal when filled in. After a minute or two, Dotty said, "I'd better go home and get ready for leaving in the morning. I hope there isn't any snow in the pass, or at least the road is bare."

"Well, I hope you guys have an enjoyable trip and fun in Denver. Call me when you get back so I can fill you in on what we did on Tuesday's meeting. I have a feeling we'll finish the puzzle. I'll keep it together until you see it completed."

"You could do that or take a picture of it. You might not want to leave it assembled. It takes a lot of table space. I'm sure Rose wants it back."

I accompanied Dotty to her car and waved as she backed out to the street. She beeped twice and sped off toward home. I returned to the puzzle. I noticed a vacancy at the lower lefthand corner and saw the piece that might fit. Would the girls be irritated with me if I found a part that filled a space? I'll try it to see if it fits. I picked up the piece. It was the right color so I tried it. It was perfect!

But should I leave it in or remove it and let someone else find it? I could put it where I would discover it when the others are present. No, I'd better not cheat. I took it back out and placed it with the scrambled pieces. Would I have been cheating? Really? I placed the cardboard transport cover over the picture and turned away from it so I wouldn't be tempted.

The weather was nasty on Saturday and Sunday, but Monday morning turned out to be a nice sunny but chilly start to the day. Frank helped me clean during Sunday. I was always proud to have a tidy home for Tuesday's club meeting. The two inches of snow from the weekend had all melted by Tuesday noon, only leaving remnants of the tiny white crystals in shady spots. I made coffee and tea for the girls and provided a plate full of assorted crackers and cheese on the dining room table, I provided a plate full of assorted crackers and cheeses..

Evie arrived first, then Sheri. We couldn't play without a fourth, so Evie, Sheri, and I sat drinking coffee and gabbing until Shannon's car showed up a few minutes after one o'clock. Sheri drifted to the front window and said, "I wonder what she is doing?"

Evie said, "What? Who?"

"Shannon's opening the trunk of her car."

"Maybe she's bringing us a cake," I joked.

"Funny, Marilee. No, it's a wheelchair. She's opening the door for Rose and helping her into the chair."

I hastily put on my coat and went out to meet them. Shannon was going to need help getting that chair lifted onto the porch and into the house. I hadn't said a word but Evie and Sheri had followed me outside. As Shannon pushed Rose toward the porch, I asked, "Did you fall, Rose?"

She looked up at me and whispered, "I'm having a little trouble getting my breath. I didn't want to miss out on the game, or I would have stayed home. Shannon borrowed a wheelchair from the hospital."

I heard her wheeze and sigh. It must have been difficult for her to have said so much. It was easy for us to elevate the chair up one step and into the living room. Four helpers provided enough muscle to make the lift. Rose gave hand signals to get her oriented at the table containing the puzzle.

I watched her whisper something to Shannon. Shannon turned to me and asked, "Rose wants to work on the puzzle. Would it be okay if I play cards?" I glanced at Sheri and Evie and they nodded their approval. I volunteered to have Shannon as my partner. Shannon asked if she could be seated so she could keep an eye on Rose. We saw nothing wrong with that arrangement and took our places.

I was pleased with the play of my partner. After four hands, we were dominating. Sheri and Evie started complaining about their consistent bad luck, so I suggested we take a break for refreshments. We helped ourselves to coffee or tea and each of us had a saucer of crackers and cheese. Shannon helped Rose with her drink. The wheelchair had a tray that extended across the mechanical arms. I had to smile as Rose pointed to certain crackers and held up fingers indicating to Shannon how many of each kind.

As we sipped and munched, we gathered around Rose at the puzzle table. Dotty, our puzzle guru, wasn't with us, but we gradually completed the puzzle except for one fairly large piece. We checked the floor, our pockets and even took all the cushions out of the furniture to search for the missing puzzle part. We never found it but we admired the puzzle even though it was incomplete.

Rose motioned to me to come closer. "I know all the pieces were in the box," she muttered. I replied, "We'll find it, Rose. Don't worry."

I spoke to the group, "Each of us has had the puzzle at our homes, so when everyone gets home, do a search for the missing fragment. It has to be somewhere. I'll search the house tonight and let you know if I find anything. I'll even check to see if Fred took it and hid it somewhere. Call me if you find it."

Evie asked me, "Have you ever known your dog to hide anything from you, Marilee?"

"Uh-huh. Food, that includes treats."

Everyone laughed.

CHAPTER 30

As we admired the gorgeous picture, I had a thought. I would have to talk with Frank about taking a vacation to the Mediterranean to visit Greece and Italy, possibly to find the location depicted in the puzzle. Someone would know the site; it must be popular.

Evie said, "Ladies, I have to return home now. I hope I'm not spoiling the game."

I checked my watch. It was almost 3:30. Two hours had passed in a flash. Evie explained, "My son is supposed to call at four about his family's Thanksgiving plans. I'd hate to listen to a recording on our answering machine. I don't get to hear his real voice very often."

Sheri asked, "Where is he calling from?"

"Toni, Terry and Tim are in New Zealand. They're going to Antarctica for a month. I wish I were going, too." Evie pulled on her coat, said "See you next week," waved and was out the door.

Sheri looked at me and shook her head. "Why would Evie want to go to Antarctica? Isn't it cold enough here in Summit's Way?"

"I think it's summer down there but I don't think they are taking their bathing suits." We both laughed as Sheri got into her winter coat. As we walked to the door, Rose called out loudly enough for us all to hear, "May I use the bathroom, Marilee?"

"Go ahead, dear."

Sheri and I watched Shannon wheel Rose down the hall to the bathroom. I didn't think much about the situation except Rose probably drank too much tea and might not make it home without having a bladder accident. I walked with Sheri out to her car talking about what an adventure to Antarctica might be like, especially flying to and from New Zealand. Sheri asked me, "Do they fly from Australia?"

"Geez, I don't know. I'll have to check on the Net. You've stimulated my little brain with several questions, Sheri."

"Mine, too." She grinned, climbed in the driver's seat, started the engine and with an arm motion, signaled goodbye as she drove away.

I scurried back to the house to see Shannon and Rose preparing to leave. "Are you going to need any help getting out to the car, Rose?"

Shannon replied, "No, we're okay. I can handle the chair going down only one step, it's easy."

Rose slowly raised her head, looked up at me and uttered, "Thank you for the good time, Marilee. We'll see you next week. I hope you find that missing puzzle piece." She smiled wanly as Shannon guided the wheelchair toward the front door. Shannon called back as they exited, "Thank you, Mrs. Neally. I loved playing bridge today."

I watched Shannon help Rose into the passenger seat, shut the door and slide the collapsed chair into the trunk. Shannon seemed to have every movement choreographed to expend the least effort. She appeared to have accepted the care of Rose as if she had been trained for the job. Perhaps Shannon had found her calling. I was proud of her.

When Frank got home and took off his coat, he stopped in front of the puzzle and admired the picture. "Very nice, Mari. You guys played bridge and finished the scene, except for one piece. Was it lost during the transporting from house to house?"

"We're looking for that piece. Everybody is going to search their cars and homes to see if they can come up with it. Rose insists that all the pieces were in the box. I'm confident that we'll find it. Rose wants to see the completed picture. We'd like to please her; she is so nice. Everyone loves her."

As Frank went to the bathroom to wash his hands, he commented, "She's very smart, too. I hope you find the piece that completes the picture."

On Friday, Frank had just left for work when the phone rang. I expected another call from the NRCC but it was Evie. The handset said Raymond Meyers.

"Hi, Evie. Did you find the missing puzzle piece?"

"No. That's not why I called. There's an ambulance at Rose's house. I thought you would like to know. There was a strange car over there yesterday. A heavyset man in a suit was inside for about an hour."

"Maybe it was a doctor. You know she hasn't been feeling well. I hope it's not serious."

"Oh Marilee, they're taking someone out on a gurney. I can't see who it is; the person is covered with a blanket. Oh! There's Shannon, so Rose must be on the gurney."

There was a lull in Evie's voice for nearly a minute.

"Are you there, Evie?"

"Yes. Shannon's coming over. She's crossing the street now. I have to put the phone down to open the door. I'll call you back."

I sat on the sofa with the phone beside me on the cushion for at least five minutes before being startled when the handset rang. I grabbed the phone after one ring.

"Hello." All I could hear was crying and sniffling. It must be Shannon; Evie wouldn't be exhibiting such behavior. "Shannon, is that you?"

"Oh, Mrs. Neally, it's so sad. Rose . . . Rose passed away in her sleep last night. What should I do now?"

"You stay with Evie. I'll be right there to talk with you. Just wait with Evie until I come over. Okay?"

"All . . . all right."

I slipped into my winter coat and flung on my scarf. I stood there next to the puzzle for a moment trying to think of what I needed with me. Purse with keys and license, that was it. I locked the kitchen door, went into the garage, climbed into my car and started toward Evie's. Instead of the zigzag path, I took the straight route, five blocks south, turn right and another five blocks. I parked at the curb and rushed to the front door where Evie greeted me.

"Come in Marilee. Shannon's really broken up about losing Rose. She's kind of lost and doesn't want to say much. Do you think she's in shock?"

"Let's see if we can get her calmed down. Can you make us some tea?"

"Sure. Here, let me take your things."

Evie put my belongings in her hall closet as I went to sit beside Shannon on the sofa. She rotated her head and looked at me, then threw her arms around my shoulders in a hug. She started crying.

I asked, "Rose had a visitor yesterday, who was that? Was it a doctor?"

"No . . . Rose told me to go into my bedroom. She told me who he was after he drove away. It was her lawyer. I don't know why he was there; she didn't say and I didn't ask."

"Hmm, maybe she had some adjustments to her will. I have a feeling she knew she was going to pass."

"I think so too, Mrs. Neally. She didn't appear well on Tuesday; kind of like she was gutting it out to be there. But she wanted to see everyone. She told me she had to be there and needed my assistance. She made me swear not to say anything about her trip to the bathroom. I promised."

I thought for a moment. "She had a secret of some sort. I wonder what she was thinking." I glanced at Shannon but she looked away and shook her head.

"I promised, Mrs. Neally."

"That's all right, Shannon. You don't have to tell me."

Evie suggested, "If you like, you can stay here tonight. I don't think you want to stay in Rose's house all alone tonight."

I acknowledged, "That's a good idea, Evie. Tomorrow will offer us some tranquility and remove much uncertainty."

"Is it all right for me to remain in Rose's house for now? I have to find another place to stay and a new job. I really liked being with Rose. She was like a mother to me. Do you think I should return to Denver to look for work?"

"I think you can stay where you are for now. Did Rose tell you the lawyer's name?"

"Yes. It's Bernard." She generated a weak smile. "When Rose told me his name, I thought she said barnyard. She laughed when I told her but that caused her to start coughing. I got her a glass of water."

Evie asked, "Can we go with you to get some of your things? If you want, you can stay here for the weekend. I'm sure by Monday things will look much better." She looked at me, "Marilee will call the lawyer for you."

"Sure, I'll call him this afternoon. He probably doesn't work on weekends; I don't think lawyers do." I stood and said, "Let's go across the street and get your things. How about the three of us having lunch together? We'll go to Conner's." Evie raised her eyebrows and nodded.

"I've never been there. My brother told me that it's a nice place to eat."

It briefly flashed through my mind what Frank might say but I refrained from mentioning cops and donuts; a comment like that would certainly be out of place. I was sincerely concerned about Shannon, the temporary fix to her employment problems had now collapsed. Without financial support from Rose, she was destined for freefall. Maybe I can suggest something for her at Conner's restaurant. I hope to get a chance to talk with Mrs. Conner. Shannon might try waitressing.

My car was facing the right direction to proceed directly to the restaurant, so I had Shannon get in the front passenger seat and Evie slid in back. I turned the key, started the heater and we were off for a nice lunch. I was eager to see Shannon enjoy a serene meal absent from thinking about the recent death of Rose. But that might be a delicate outcome. We decided to retrieve Shannon's things after returning from Conner's.

It was almost noon when I turned into the restaurant's parking area. I parked beside a dark maroon BMW sedan. As we got out of my car, Shannon commented, "I think this is Mr. Bernard's car. He must be here for lunch, too."

When Evie joined us, she stated, "Let's go inside and find a good seat near the windows. I'd like to see how the town looks during daylight."

Shannon followed her closely and I trailed a bit behind her, scanning for Mrs. Conner. No greeters were present, so we seated ourselves. Shannon pointed to a man sitting by himself. "That's the lawyer, Mr. Barnyard." She placed her hand over her mouth and shyly giggled. Her depression had evidently cleared appreciably. Evie's suggestion to come to Conner's had gotten us away from Rose's dwelling to a more agreeable environment for Shannon.

I glanced at the well-dressed man wondering if I should speak to him about Rose's passing. I decided against the idea. I looked away and noticed Mrs. Conner approaching our table with a tray of water glasses.

After placing orders, we babbled for a minute or so before Mr. Bernard stood and approached our table. I had never seen him before, so I was sure he didn't recognize me. It must be Shannon or maybe Evie.

"Excuse me, ladies. Sorry to interrupt. I'm Cecil Bernard, Rose Toliver's lawyer." He nodded to Shannon. "About an hour ago, I heard

Rose had passed. I'm so sorry. She was a grand lady. I assume you are all Rose's friends."

I observed him staring at Evie. "Oh, you are Mrs. Meyers. We haven't met but I recognize you from your picture on your husband's desk at the bank. I met Shannon yesterday, but I haven't met you."

He looked straight at me and I introduced myself, "I'm Marilee Neally."

"Oh, sure. Your husband runs the post office."

"That's right. Would you like to join us, Mr. Bernard?"

He looked back at his table. His food hadn't been delivered yet. "Thank you. I'd like that. You are all mentioned in Rose's will. I can give you some information."

I reacted, "We're mentioned in her will?"

"Yes, ma'am. Shannon and the bridge club members are all designated as beneficiaries. Miss Rose wanted you all to gather at Mrs. Neally's home for reading of the will. She wanted the reading to be carried out as soon as possible following her death. I understand the bridge club normally meets on Tuesdays. Would that be convenient for you ladies?"

"We'd normally be meeting at Dorthy Higgins', but I guess we can convene at my home for the reading. We can call Dorthy and Sheri. I'm sure they will agree to the unusual meeting, considering it was Rose's wish."

"Fine. I will schedule the reading of Rose Toliver's will this coming Tuesday at 2:00 p.m. Please let me know if that is an inconvenient time for anyone."

Two waiters delivered our lunch and we shared anecdotes about Rose while we ate. Some of the stories were from other sources and we had no way to verify them, but knowing about Rose and her benevolence, we tended to believe the tales.

Our food and conversation ended at a quarter to two. We said goodbye to Mr. Bernard and drove back to Evie's. Evie made calls to Dotty and Sheri informing them about the reading of Rose's will at my home on Tuesday. They promised to be there even if inclement weather caused major problems. Following the calls, Evie and I went across the street with Shannon to assist her with things she needed for the weekend. She packed a small suitcase with the items, just enough for two days.

CHAPTER 31

Over the weekend, my bridge buddies reported they had searched from cellar to attic for that missing chunk of puzzle with no success. I had done the same, finding nothing but a few items I had misplaced, thinking they were lost.

Each day until Tuesday I sporadically speculated why Rose wanted us to meet at my home for the reading of her will. But I didn't lose any sleep thinking about it and finally concluded she was giving us her books on bridge, astronomy, and her old, nearly forgotten stamp collection. I couldn't imagine what she had instore for Shannon, having known her for only a few weeks.

During breakfast Tuesday morning Frank suggested Rose was bequeathing each of us an antique of some sort. I didn't think much of that idea. I had never observed any antiques when visiting Rose. She told us she had a closet full of old clothes that she never wore. Maybe we were to be asked to dispose of them at church or Good Will.

At one-thirty I started Mr. Coffee and our old coffee maker to prepare plenty of fresh brew. I made sure I had at least six sparkling clean cups and mugs ready. I opened a family size package of oatmeal cookies and piled them on a large plate. I was ready. When the doorbell rang, I swept past the puzzle, glanced at that spot for the missing piece and wondered if it would ever be found.

Evie, Sheri and Mr. Bernard were waiting on the porch, having arrived almost simultaneously. Mr. Bernard held a small black briefcase. I let them in and introduced Sheri to the lawyer. As I was closing the door, Dotty and Shannon arrived. They didn't have to knock or ring the bell; I quickly opened the door so they could rush inside to avoid the gusting cold northern wind carrying a few tiny snowflakes. It felt like the white stuff was on the way in large amounts this time.

I was going to introduce Dotty to Cecil Bernard, but they were conversing as if they were old friends, so I didn't bother. I suggested everyone sit at the dining room table. Those that wanted coffee and a cookie helped themselves and took a seat. The scene resembled a small company's conference meeting with all eyes focused on the CEO, Rose's lawyer.

Mr. Bernard opened his briefcase and withdrew some papers held together with a paper clip. I noticed the embossed seal of a notary public. He surveyed our faces and asked, "Are you ready for me to read Rose Toliver's will?"

There wasn't a sound but we all nodded.

He began, "I Rose Meridith Toliver, of sound mind and body do hereby bequeath the following: 1. To the ladies of the bridge club, all my books concerning the game of bridge. There are about twenty of them. I so enjoyed your accepting me into your group, though for only a short time. 2. To dear Shannon Durham, I leave my savings account of approximately twenty thousand dollars and my home. Mr. Bernard will guide you through the paperwork. Please use the money to further your education or training. 3. To Mrs. Neally I leave my stamp collection so her husband can sell it for a contribution to the observatory and this envelope. Marilee, you will know what to do when you open the cover. Those are my last wishes, Rose M. Toliver."

Tears began cascading down Shannon's cheeks. She uttered, "Oh, my gosh. She has turned my life around! I can never thank her enough."

Mr. Bernard handed me a small white envelope with my name written on the face. Everyone was watching as I tore open the paper cover and found a small piece of posterboard. I frowned as I inspected the heavy paper. I flipped it over and found a nickel taped to it. I held it up for all to see.

Evie was the first to react. "What does that mean, Marilee?"

Sheri added, "Well, it's not a penny for her thoughts."

Dotty chuckled, "That's inflation for you, ladies and gentleman."

"I know exactly what it means. Please wait a minute while I go to my scale by the bathroom. Shannon, please come with me."

I had to have help to move the scale away from the wall so I could get to the back panel. I had a hunch Shannon had done it before. She wiped her face with a cloth napkin and followed me to the nook outside the bathroom. I asked her, "Can you pull the scale into the hallway so I can get to the back?"

She tipped the scale a little bit and rotated it into the hall. That motion verified what I thought, she had performed the operation before. I dropped the nickel in the penny slot, heard the odd metallic sound and caught the panel when it popped open. I put my right hand inside the opening and felt for a gun, any object. Nothing. So, whatever I was supposed to find must be in the coin catching receptacle. I extracted it from the scale and carried it back to the dining room. I guessed what Rose wanted me to find must be in with the jumble of coins, perhaps a rare one.

I set the container on the table and commented, "I'm not sure what I'm looking for but it must be in this little cardboard box." I poured the cluster of pennies on the table. Sheri pointed and exclaimed, "Look! Something's taped to the bottom of the box!"

My hand was partially covering the bottom of the container. I removed my hand and saw it! I could tell by the shape; it was the missing puzzle piece, the last piece. The shape of that puzzle piece was etched into my brain. I peeled off the tape and made my way to the puzzle. The noises from the chairs scooting back had no effect on me. I inserted the piece into the puzzle and was amazed at what I saw, Rose Toliver's signature, 1958. Rose painted the picture in 1958 and was a real artist. Why had she kept her artistic talents from us? Maybe Shannon can explain Rose's secrecy.

We were amazed at what had been revealed, except for Shannon. She remained at the dining table talking with Mr. Bernard. I assumed they were discussing the legalities of ownership of the house and the money she was to receive. As Mr. Bernard picked up his things and prepared to leave, he stopped to look at the puzzle and commented, "Rose was quite a talented artist, wasn't she?"

Each of us shook hands with Mr. Bernard, thanking him for reading the will. He left us to admire the puzzle and talk about Rose's last requests. Evie and I started back to the table where Shannon sat, nursing her cup of coffee. She was deep in thought and came out of her daze when the group joined her.

I had to ask her about the formerly missing puzzle piece. What could she tell us and not violate any promises made to Rose? "Shannon, can you explain what Rose was thinking?"

She hesitated, then nodded. "I can now tell you some things since you've found the last piece. She didn't want me to say anything until you had the puzzle completed."

Dotty inquired, "Did she have a reason to keep us from knowing she was the puzzle picture artist?"

"Not really. When she was growing up she was very mischievous. She was a lonely child and loved to play tricks on people, especially other youngsters. She loved to read and got involved with books as soon as she could visit the library by herself. She found that books helped unite people and when she met you ladies, she though you needed to be united, more than playing cards together..

"She gave you the puzzle without one piece to see if you would work together. When you started the vigilante group, she decided the missing puzzle piece wasn't necessary. You were all working toward a goal. But then she fell ill and I helped her hide the puzzle piece in the scale. She had a feeling that she wouldn't be with us much longer. I was surprised when she passed away so soon. We were getting along so well, I hoped to learn more from her. She was a great teacher, better than I ever had in school."

"But what about her artistic work? She had the painting made into a puzzle."

"She studied art but realized early on that she could never make a living with art, but she could almost always find a job as a librarian. With books all around her, she could learn about anything that interested her. She loved astronomy and even science fiction."

Shannon seemed to have become more outgoing and reassured. In the short time she lived with Rose, this unsure and defeated young woman had blossomed.

As I surveyed my friends, I realized we had all benefited by knowing Rose. She had bettered all our lives, even Frank's.